VINDICATED

A Novel of Mary Shelley

Kathleen Williams Renk

Cuidono • Brooklyn

Vindicated

ISBN: 978-1-944453-10-7

eISBN: 978-1-944453-11-4

Cover Image: Unknown Woman, formerly known as Mary Shelley
Samuel John Stump, 1831 ©National Portrait Gallery, London

Cuidono Press
Brooklyn NY
www.cuidono.com

For my daughter, Sarah,
and for my granddaughters
Maeve, Piper, Carrigan
Isabella and Sloane

PROLOGUE

1797

I hear them murmur, "Bring in the pups to suckle. Perhaps that will loosen the afterbirth." I want to shout "No! Bring me my baby," but my tongue is tied. I am hot and thirsty, but no one offers me water. "Please," I beg them in my mind. And then nothing. I drift out of my body. I search for my daughter.

31 August 1797

Even though we have prestigious surgeons in attendance, I begin to think that these surgeons are fools. One wears his powdered wig askew, looking like a pantaloon. I inquire what their objective is in healing my dear wife Mary, and all they say is that they need to remove the remainder of the afterbirth, which is stuck. They think that bringing pups to suck on my wife's breasts may make her womb contract sufficiently to release the last bits of the placenta, and thus cure her of her fever and blood poisoning. I watch incredulously as they try to coax the pups to nurse on the human teat. If Mary were truly here in full force, if she were cognizant, she would be appalled and would be calling the surgeons out for their ludicrous plan. I feel such shock in seeing my brilliant wife so lethargic and ill that I suffer mental paralysis in regard to the correct course of action. I try to believe that the surgeons possess reason and logic and know precisely what they are doing. I must have faith in their abilities and knowledge. Surely they have seen other such cases and understand the remedy.

I briefly consult with the head doctor, Dr. George Fordyce, a friend and expert whom Mary insisted on procuring, and ask him why he doesn't place the newborn child at the breast, instead of these ridiculous pups. He says that without the mother's guidance the child cannot latch on. The pups know instinctively what to do. Is he suggesting that humans possess less instinct than other animals? I wonder what Erasmus Darwin would say in response to his absurd and unsubstantiated claim.

So far, I don't see any progress. The puppies just lie on Mary's chest, which heaves with each breath. They do not root for the teat. They snuggle next to each other, while the surgeons take turns tickling their feet to entice them to nurse. If this weren't so very tragic, the scene would be comical. The midwife, Mrs. Blenkinsop, stands in the background with her arms folded across her chest. She remains silent because she knows that these foolish men will not ask for or listen to her expert advice, even though she is the head midwife at Westminster Lying-In Hospital and has personally attended more births than all of these buffoons combined. She seems as disgusted and baffled as I am.

4 September 1797

It's now been five days since Mary gave birth to our daughter, her namesake. During her early labor, she was cheerful and felt well enough to write notes, three of which she scribbled to me for I had gone, as was my habit, to my apartments to read Greek and Latin. As per her routine each morning, she sat in the parlor and read the *Times*. In a note addressed to me, she informed me that she had sent for Mrs. Blenkinsop because her labor had begun but she joked that the "animal will not arrive today." She cuddled with little Fanny and told her that she would soon have a baby sister or brother to hold. When the pains became difficult to ignore, Mrs. Blenkinsop escorted my wife up to her bed chamber.

Now, my wife drifts in and out of consciousness due to her trauma. Periodically, it seems as though she is about to turn a corner and be ready to take on the task of mothering our miniature Mary. During her lucid periods, she has asked to see the child but the surgeons believe that it would do more harm than good, that she will experience the stress of motherhood when she ought to focus her mind and soul on healing her womb. It seems strange to me that men who believe that women are mere wombs and mothers at heart don't see any efficacy in Mary succoring her child. Surely a child sucking at her mother's breast would have greater benefit than these ineffective, preposterous puppies. And Mary is an excellent mother with experience in caring for her first-born, Fanny, but also in writing about how one should raise and educate daughters in a modern, liberal way, to allow them to flourish in reason and brilliance in the way that males are encouraged and permitted to do. In observing her struggle, I fear that she may not live long enough to educate her daughters and watch them grow to womanhood.

As I watch my wife, I fret about what life may be like, if she does not recover. What if she is an invalid? Or worse yet, what if she succumbs to the toxin that poisons her? Sometimes I think that I should have studied medicine rather than philosophy so that I could better assist her in her time of need.

❧

I felt better briefly and asked to see my child but the surgeons forbade it. The doctors say that I am too weak to hold the child because I have lost a river of blood. I vaguely recall seeing the blood rush out all over the bed. I felt Mrs. Blenkinsop lift my hips and place pillows beneath them in order to stop the hemorrhaging. I felt her vigorously rub the top of my womb until it cramped and became hard like a rock. But then I lost consciousness and drifted away.

I want to see my Mary. I don't even know what she looks like, if she looks like William or me, or a combination of us. Does she have my auburn hair? I wonder what sort of person she will become and if she will possess William's superior intelligence and my stubborn tenacity. When the surgeons were out of my sick room, I asked Mrs. Blenkinsop to bring my baby to me and she pledged that she would. "I give you my word, Mistress Mary," she said. I have known Mrs. Blenkinsop all these many months and I fully believe that she will fulfill her promise. I trusted her to deliver my baby and to bring in a doctor, if needed, which she did when the afterbirth failed to release on its own. She is a reliable woman who possesses excellent midwifery and childcare knowledge and knows that it is crucial for the mother and child to grow close. I fear that the child will not know me and when I am well, she won't latch on and feed properly.

I just want to touch her and know that she is real. That I didn't dream her into being. I felt something on my chest periodically and weakly sucking at my bosom. I assume that the surgeons relented or that Mrs. Blenkinsop did her duty to me and brought my child to my breast for the child's nourishment and for my emotional and physical well-being.

5 September 1797

This evening my Mary experienced a shaking spell that went on for what seemed like hours. Her teeth chattered; her whole body shook; the bed trembled below her. Mrs. Blenkinsop fetched as many counterpanes as she could find and piled them on Mary. She heated water and placed it in a hot-water bottle to warm the bed as they do in Scotland, her homeland. She fetched more logs and then stoked the fire in the fireplace. I blame Mary's shivering in part on this old, drafty house built right after the Great Fire of London. The wind whistles through every crack in the window sashes and even roars down the chimney; we can't keep the fire lit.

Mary looked so distressed and kept repeating, "I am so cold, William. Please do something. I fear I should die." I crawled under the counterpanes with her and held her in my arms, but she shook so violently that I feared she would have a seizure. I tried to keep her from thrashing about. Finally, she came to rest in my arms. Mrs. Blenkinsop placed a cold compress on Mary's forehead and I continued to hold her, hoping that my action gave her some comfort. I watched her chest rise and fall to ensure that she was still with us, still breathing.

If she quakes again, the surgeons threaten leeches and cupping.

ଔ

I am not a believer in a patriarchal god and neither is William, even though he is an ordained minister as was his father, but the world feels strange to me right now because I believe that

I have seen glimpses of an afterlife where my mother Elizabeth is. She beckons me to join her. It's odd because I was fully awake when this occurred; I wasn't dreaming. I shook my head when she gestured to me to cross over and meet her. I tacitly told her that I still have work to do here, to help my wee daughters and to work on behalf of all women. We are just beginning to make some progress towards the idea that women should not be treated as overgrown children, that we have the right to be educated and to be treated, not as dolls for men's amusement, but as full and complete human beings, not imperfect men or half-formed creatures. I don't wish to depart this life for another, assuming that there is another world in which to reside. For now, my mother seemed satisfied when I explained my reasoning. She seemed to be able to read my mind. She has not departed though; she stands on the edge of my lying-in room, and patiently waits.

Oddly, my mother has disappeared and my beloved Fanny Blood has appeared in her place. Perhaps my mother convinced Fanny to try to persuade me to join them. I nursed and attempted to minister to Fanny in Portugal during her confinement. Tragically and regretfully, I was unsuccessful in my practice. My poor Fanny, who was a great soul, hemorrhaged right in front of me. Blood, just like her name, gushed forth and flooded the bed, like an overflowing fountain. I could do nothing to stop it, even when the midwife compressed and robustly rubbed the top of the womb as is necessary following birth. The bleeding did not cease and Fanny turned as white as alabaster. Then her heart gave out and stopped beating.

Fanny is certainly not here to nurse me; clearly, she is my Fetch. She stands wrapped in her shroud with her hands extended toward me, pleading with me to go with her to help her find her baby girl. She repeats over and over that her child is hungry and is crying for her. She doesn't seem to realize that her child was born too early and never took a breath.

I feel helpless and all that I can say is, "Forgive me, Fanny. I did what I could, but I didn't have the skill to save you or your babe." I try to reassure her that her child is at peace. I fear Fanny's presence and her reprimand, her scowling look, which she never once exhibited in real life towards me. In life, she was my dearest and most admired friend. I looked up to her.

I don't believe in Fate or in what the Hindus call karma, but Fanny seems to be a testament to what is in store for me. She persists, despite my entreaties. I ask her to please leave me or, if she can't, to not stand so close and accuse me of her death or to beg me to go with her; I am not prepared and I don't wish to leave Godwin and my daughters.

I did my best for Fanny while she was dying and tried to comfort her in her final hours, just as I had attempted to save other women, my mother when she was tyrannized by my ruthless father, my sister Eliza whom I helped escape from her cruel and heartless husband, Mr. Bishop, my pupils in Ireland, Lady Kingsborough's girls, who were being raised to be decorative, brainless "ladies." I have tried to intervene on behalf of the women and girls in my life and for all women. I may not have always been consistent; sometimes I despaired and was weak. I profoundly regret that I tried twice to throw away my life. How horribly ironic that I now cling to and beg for it.

I wish that women could help me, but all I have are men encircling me who seem not to know what to do to save me. They speak to each other in hushed tones and act as though I am already deceased. Sometimes they chuckle and pass the brandy bottle around to one another. They seem tipsy as they discuss their clubs and polo matches. Mrs. Blenkinsop would help me, if she could, but she is completely outnumbered and dominated by foolish men.

The one doctor that Godwin called in at my behest, Dr. Fordyce, confirmed that Dr. Poingnand created this catastrophe in not removing the placenta intact but rather in pieces, like a jigsaw puzzle. Mrs. Blenkinsop called him in to attend me after the birth, when the afterbirth failed to expel. Unfortunately, he had just come from a rather messy autopsy of a convict, a true rogue he said. Mrs. Blenkinsop noticed blood on the doctor's hands and offered him water to rinse them but he said, "That's completely unnecessary. A little blood never hurt anyone. Besides," he said, "I need to get to my club. Now, let's see what we have here." He reached inside me and gave a swift tug on the umbilical cord. I felt something rip and then I saw him pull pieces of the placenta from my womb, one by one. He handed them off to Mrs. Blenkinsop who held out a large basin to receive them. He tried to reconstruct the afterbirth in the basin but saw that parts of it were missing. Some remained clinging to my womb and he had no idea how to get them out. After that, Godwin did require that Dr. Poingnand stop attending me, but the other doctors who have replaced him, even my friend Fordyce, prove that they are as incompetent.

I saw the pieces of the afterbirth lying in a bowl; they looked like large, grotesque pieces of purple liver. I have read that in some aboriginal societies, women eat their afterbirths, just as animals do. If it would save me so that I could properly mother my child, I'd undertake this repulsive act.

VINDICATED

A new doctor is in attendance, Mr. Carlisle. He has ordered a diet of wine for Mary and has instructed me to dose her with it liberally. Mary has never been an imbiber of spirits; her father was a drunkard, a true dipsomaniac, and she saw the disastrous consequences of intemperance. She even considered brandy a bane and rightly surmised that intoxication contributes to social disease and the physical and emotional abuse of women and children.

Initially, she adamantly refused the wine, but I told her expressly that Mr. Carlisle believes that it will relieve her of her malady. "Why does he want me drunk?" Mary asked.

I wasn't sure, but I fabricated a reply. "Perhaps he thinks that the wine will relax you sufficiently so that you will let go of the last bits of afterbirth."

Of course, I didn't nor did Mary believe that she had mental control of this malady. Yet we were desperate and Mary relented and allowed me to pour tumbler after tumbler, all in the hopes that she would be cured of this toxin that persists despite all attempts to destroy it. The only effect of the misguided remedy was complete and utter stupor.

I have lost all faith in these doctors; I wanted to believe that they know what is best, that they are experts in childbirth and its complications, but surely there must be something beyond drunken stupor that can cure my wife who becomes more and more of an invalid with each passing day. I grow angry and curse the universe but find that there is nothing that I can do but hold on to the hope that she will rise, like Jarius's daughter or Lazarus, from her death bed and be my wife and companion again. I flirt with the idea of firing the entire lot of doctors, of turning the case over to Mrs. Blenkinsop alone. Surely, a woman can discern what the remedy is, not men who have never conceived a child or given birth.

᧖ᦷ

Godwin spoke to me today in cloaked sentences, never revealing what he truly thinks. He asked me, "What do you want for your children, your daughters?" I knew exactly what he meant. He believes that I am on the verge of death and wants to know what I want done with the children. Surely he must know. Of course, I want my girls to live with him and to be educated as equals to men, but I despair because he seems to imply that there is no hope for me. I am doomed. I can see it in his eyes, even though he does not allow the words to issue from his mouth. I did not answer his question but turned my face to the wall.

Fanny Blood lingers at the foot of my bed, wrapped in her shroud. She holds two half-pennies in her hand; she's ready to place them on my eyes. "No," I shout. I am not ready. I am not willing. I am only 38 years old. I have not accomplished all that I wish to accomplish. I have not won a great victory for humanity, for women, half of the world's citizens. If I had, perhaps I would be content to surrender to death. And I am not ready to abandon my poor daughters who will never know the depth of my love and affection for them.

I cannot bear to think of being no more. It seems impossible that I should cease to exist.

9 September 1797

My dear wife's faculties have decayed; she appears to hallucinate and talks to people who are not there. She mumbles something nonsensical about her childhood friend Fanny Blood and dead babies. Occasionally, she comes out of her stupor and asks to see the child, but Dr. Fordyce still prohibits it.

I waited until Dr. Fordyce departed for his club and I asked Mrs. Blenkinsop to fetch the child. Mrs. Blenkinsop and I consulted; she thinks that this is the best way to heal my wife and relieve her of this ordeal. The child's hunger will be Mary's salvation.

We had to shake Mary to awaken her; she seemed to have entered another realm. However, when she saw her namesake, she became alert and gathered her to her breast. She seemed herself again and I had to restrain myself from weeping like a child. I swallowed tears as Mary, my darling wife, held our daughter, cradling her next to her bosom and whispering endearments to her. "Mon petit chou, mon coeur." The child seemed famished and nursed readily, emptying my wife's breasts and relieving her of pain. The child continued to suck and fell asleep as did Mary. She was finally at peace. For the first time, I felt hopeful. Mrs. Blenkinsop will bring the child to Mary in another two hours. The doctors be damned. Now, we wait to see if the last bits of afterbirth will pass. Perhaps the child will save, will resurrect, my dear wife.

I dreamt that my new daughter was brought to me. It sounds odd that in looking at her diminutive face I could see that she will become what I wish for her to be. She has a broad forehead like Godwin, which indicates a capacious, philosophical mind. For a moment, I could visualize her beating heart and I could see that it will be filled with passion but also reasoned sensibility. I only hope that her lust for life will not impede all that she can become; I don't want her to make the same mistakes that I did and fall in love with an unworthy, unfaithful man. I ardently wish that I could remain in this world to see her grow into a woman, a full human being.

Godwin brought Fanny in to say her goodbyes. She is still my love-child, named after my first love, Fanny Blood. I've tried my best to forget about little Fanny's father, Gilbert Imlay, the man who wrecked my heart, who caused me irreparable heartache. *Whatever happens, she is testament to my enduring love for him, even despite his cruelty and duplicity to me.* Godwin cannot know that Imlay still resides in my heart as I approach my end.

After little Fanny returned to her nursery, Fanny Blood came closer and sat next to me on my bed. She unwrapped her shroud and placed the corner of it in my hand and then laid her cold hand in mine. Our fingers intertwined. She no longer looked angry with me. I even saw a shy smile grace her lips. I nodded to affirm my love for her.

10 September 1797

It is over. Mary labored to breathe for nearly three hours this morning. Her pulse was erratic and the doctors often thought that she was gone but then she would rise up and gasp as if she was trying her best to stay here in this world with us. Finally, at 7:40, the struggle was over and her spirit departed.

I blame these inept doctors who know so little about how to contain life. And the child herself failed to save the only woman that I have ever truly loved. In fact, some would say that the child killed her mother. This is what the dressers whispered as they washed my wife's body and prepared her for burial. I had to close my ears to their words, even though, in a sense, they are true. I shall endeavor not to blame young Mary; she will need my affection and devotion and, in a way, she will need to serve as her mother's replacement, if that is possible.

I am numb. Eleven days ago, we were over-joyed that our new little Mary was born. Now, my wife lies inert and cold. The light vanished from her eyes. The daring mind disappeared forever, except through the writings that she left for posterity. I will remain faithful to her memory and ensure that she is not forgotten.

15 September 1797

Today we buried Mary Wollstonecraft, the author of *A Vindication of the Rights of Woman*, at St. Pancras Church, Middlesex, the church where we were joyfully wed five months ago. I must return home and leave my wife in the ground. I have two young daughters who need their mother. All that they have is me, an old Prospero, who wishes to bury himself in his books. I need to return to my study and sort out how to proceed in this life without the person for whom I felt the greatest affinity and ardor. The person who gave me my first taste of genuine love and life.

1811

Tragically, I never knew my mother. Nevertheless, she haunts my waking and dreaming worlds.

Like God, my father forbade me from eating from the tree of knowledge of good and evil. He encouraged me to read everything that my philosopher mother had penned but did not permit me to read the memoir that he had written about my mother after I killed her.

One evening, after one of our rows, my stepmother, Mrs. Clairmont, announced that it was time I learned my origin and she handed me the outlawed book that included an account of my mother's death. I read it and then I stayed up until my candle burned all the way down and imagined what my mother and my father may have thought and felt during Mother's last days, days that forever changed the course of my own life. Thus, I returned to my origins for it is sometimes said that a mother's life ends when a child is born. In this case, that is literally true.

Right now, I am fourteen years old. I endeavor to be close to my mother Mary by visiting her grave and resting against her tombstone while I learn from her by re-reading her writings and what my father wrote about her after she died. I feel such guilt that my birth effected the end of a modern Hypatia, a brilliant female philosopher who advocated for women's rights, a champion for women and girls who told women the truth—that their minds are "enfeebled by false refinement"—that they are rational beings, like men—that they have the right to be educated in the same way as males are. The "organ" that nourished me in her womb, essentially a part of myself, and the cord that connected me to my mother, extinguished my mother's life. That seems so ironic and obviously tragic. Something straight out of Sophocles. Whenever I read or hear the story of her gruesome and untimely death, I cover my eyes and ears so that I feel less responsible for killing my mother. I feel shame. My father has lamented that I failed to save my mother, but I dare not ask what that even means. How can a newborn child possibly save her mother?

I often sit and gaze for hours at my mother's portrait, which hangs above the fireplace in Father's study. Father commissioned it after my mother died. She looks so wise and learned, as if she is a great counselor of all women and men, as if she could be one of Plato's Guardians in his *Republic*. I speak with her and disclose my heart to her, telling her how I wish she could return to earth, telling her that I wish that she could tell me her own life story. She remains silent and stoic, though, and I am forced to turn to her writing to hear her words.

Some believe that her *Mary: A Fiction* is a thinly-veiled autobiography. I do not. From the outset, my mother calls it a fiction, so obviously, she utilized her imagination in shaping her characters: Eliza, Mary, and Ann. Her only "memoir" is what my father recollected and recorded after her death. However, I can't help but think that second-hand knowledge of a life is not as accurate or meaningful as knowledge from the primary source. What if he misremembered their conversations or skewed her story in a certain way? What if she kept secret that which she wished to remain private? What if he didn't know the entire truth? And how could he, since he was not witness to many of the events? If I should ever become as famous—or infamous—as my mother, I will be sure to record my own truth so that no one makes my story their own. To that end, I shall endeavor to keep a journal so that I can record events and express my musings and thoughts as they arise.

My mother never explicitly inscribed her own story, except in her travels to Sweden, Norway, and Denmark, which she undertook alone with her maid, Marguerite, and with my half-sister Fanny when she was a baby. It was an unheard of journey for a woman alone, one thought preposterous and dangerous. But, as she did in her writing, she always demonstrated courage and daring. I hope that I have inherited these attributes of hers. I shall not dwell on the fact that she initially undertook the journey to impress and try to win back the heart of her love at the time, Mr. Gilbert Imlay, Fanny's father.

My father's memoir of my mother's early life is all that I have, so I will relate what I know from his rendition, but I may, along the way, ponder what he has said and try to imagine my ghostly mother's life.

29 December 1811

I often wonder where my mother's splendid and audacious mind came from. Her father Edward was not raised or educated to any particular profession, but, according to what my mother told Godwin, her father dallied as an itinerate farmer, moving frequently from Epping Forest to Beverley in Yorkshire to the outskirts of London to Wales and sundry other locations. Unfortunately, he was not a good, kindly man, someone to emulate. He tended toward despotic behavior, lording over the entire family, her five brothers and sisters, but most particularly over her mother.

My mother's early life was radically different from mine. Out of necessity and because she was courageous, she protected her mother from her father's wrath. I've never needed to intervene to keep my father from throttling my stepmother, although my father Godwin does, on occasion, become rather impatient and perturbed with Mrs. Clairmont, just as I do, for she can be most vindictive. When he does, he just retreats into his study to read Heraclites or further ponder his own *Political Justice*. (I, on the other hand, try to ignore her resentment of me brought on by the fact that my father adores me and I him. She's a bit of a jealous shrew, which I realize is rather unkind of me, but there it is).

Father reports that my mother was a brave soul who would stand between her intoxicated father and her mother and tell him that if he wanted to hit someone, hit her. He often complied. She accepted the blows on her mother's behalf; her face and body were bruised and blackened; she suffered broken bones. She acted as her mother's savior, unlike me. I failed as my mother's redeemer.

I would suspect that, in such circumstances, you would need to sleep with one "eye open," always concerned about potential violence. Such is the plight of woman in these times, where a man has the right to beat his wife and children without recourse, according to the "rule of thumb." We are his property. As my mother effectively argues, "A wife being as much a man's property as his horse, or his ass, she has nothing she can call her own." Not even herself, unless she claims self-ownership.

Fortunately, Godwin is not a violent or aggressive man. But, if he did strike me, I would seriously consider returning the blow. I am a pacifist, but I will defend myself, if need be. As a woman, I will own myself, as my mother advised in her writings.

With that said concerning her father's violence toward her, my Grandfather Edward made a fortunate move that benefited my mother's mind and spirit. At one point, the family moved near a Mr. Clare, a clergyman, with whom my mother spent many happy and fruitful hours. Mr. Clare was a recluse but he took a shining to my mother because he observed her quick and curious mind. Due to her inquisitive intellect and her hunger for knowledge, he generously provided her with books, the usual that any literate person would own at the time: Bunyan's *Pilgrim's Progress,* a copy of the Bible, but also Mr. Milton's *Paradise Lost.* Even though she later disparaged its supposed "sublimity," she loved its wayward Eve who longed to fly across the earth and observe with the eye of a god the entirety of the planet. Without knowing it, Mr. Clare piqued my mother's imagination, something sorely feared by the Anglican Church, allowing her to see that it may be possible for a woman to rise above her supposed station and see as a god. The only problem being that, if a woman did so, she would be condemned for her transgression and blamed, like Eve and Pandora, for unleashing all of the evils of the world. That, apparently, did not deter my mother from dreaming. She did not abide by Milton's Raphael's order to Adam and Eve to "dream not of other worlds." She imagined and believed in the possibility of a more just and perfect world for everyone but particularly for women, half of our planet's population.

So, even though Mr. Clare intended Christian instruction in his tutelage of my mother, his patronage of her mind led her to want more. Around this time, Mr. Clare introduced my mother to Frances Blood, or Fanny as she was called, and my mother grew to love this older girl who inspired her to excel. She and Fanny did not live in the same vicinity but they kept regular and lively correspondence and dreamt of the time when they would start their own school and would educate girls in the same way that boys were educated. They practiced, with the help of Mr. Clare, their Greek and Latin; they pursued mathematics; they read philosophers, like Plato, who argued that the sexes were equal, and even Aristotle, who disparaged women and believed that we are imperfect men. They knew that we are not imperfect men and that in order to become the social and political equals of men, we need the same educational opportunities. They were not discouraged or dissuaded when their fathers told them that they would not succeed in their endeavors to be published writers or to be properly educated. That they would never be vindicated in seeking an equal education or ways to use their innate talents and imaginations. That they could never be scientists, intellectuals, or philosophers. That they were wasting their time and should look to be satisfied with the domestic not public sphere; they should be content with being proper wives and mothers; this should be their singular occupation. This is what God intended for them; they should remain silent and subservient as St. Paul admonishes.

My grandfather only hoped that his daughter would marry well and become a helpmate for a successful man. However, my mother and Fanny were not content to be silent and conventional like other girls, to practice piano or fine embroidery or landscape painting or a modicum of French, in order to become "accomplished" and win a mate who would make them mute, decorative objects, like the dolls that they were supposed to have loved and cared for as they imitated motherhood. I am proud to learn that, according to Godwin, my mother refused to play with dolls as a child. She tossed them on the ground. Instead, I imagine that she ran about the farm with her brothers, climbed trees, swam in the brook, and scribbled in a discarded notebook that her father no longer used. Her childish writings intermingled with the cost of pig feed and when to begin the harvest.

I have been far more fortunate in my education. Although I have not been formally educated, as privileged boys are at elite schools, because girls are not allowed to attend Harrow or Eton or any of the public schools that lead to Oxford or Cambridge, Godwin has educated me and given me every available material mental object; he made his vast library available to me and my sister Fanny, although she is not as inclined to burrow into a chair and read Dante's *Paradiso* as I am. My father has attempted to raise me in the fashion that my mother describes in her "Thoughts on the Education of Daughters," which I have pored through to try to absorb what she hoped for me, Fanny, and all girls.

I do wish that I had been suckled by my mother, as Fanny was, and not a wet nurse; my mother feared wet nurses who could pass on syphilis and other venereal diseases in their breast milk! Fortunately, my father followed my mother's prescriptions and was careful to choose a healthy wet nurse; I suffered no ill effects from being fed by her. In my mother's book, my mother advocated mother's milk and a mother's tenderness as the first way that a child learns about love. Godwin, of course, could not provide this mother's milk but he tried to ensure that my wet nurse and nursery nurse were not ignorant or given to allowing me to exercise all of my passions, but rather cultivate my reason.

My nursery nurse read to me and Godwin did too, in the way that my mother professed. Later he instructed my stepmother in these methods, although she was not a tender reader or teacher. I find this odd, since she and my father are now publishing children's books. At any rate, first, I was read stories about animals, like "The Perambulation of the Mouse," to cultivate my heart and then later stories of experiences of nature and its innate beauties, rather than absurd fairy stories. Godwin, like my mother, forbids ridiculous fairy tales that foster female dependence.

He also affirms, like my mother, that ostentatious dress and cosmetics "enfeeble" women and hide the true nature of the human being. I once saw a woman riding in a carriage with blue and red powder in her hair, her face painted white, as if she were dead. I told Godwin that she looked like the living dead, a zombie that my Jamaican nursery nurse, Miss Adela, told me about! My father laughed at my assumption and said that her look was deliberate and supposedly fashionable and that such face paint contains arsenic, a poison, which, of course, cannot be good for the complexion and can be fatal for the body. He said that my mother also criticized this artificiality. Yet it was difficult not to look at the spectacle of this woman seeking so much vain attention for herself. I wondered if she knew that poison was seeping into her blood as she smiled her vacuous smile. Although I am not given to vanity, there may come a time when it will behoove me to wear such face paint, to don the look of a zombie. If I need to, I will, but I will retain within me my inherent self-worth and not lose my soul in the process.

30 December 1811

I have also been fortunate that Godwin has included me in his "circle of friends," even though I am too young to fully take part.

VINDICATED

As a child, I often listened with Fanny from the stairs or under the table to the boisterous arguments rendered by his friends about reason vs. passion, good government, and human perfectibility. For the entirety of my life, we have been frequently visited by intellectuals: economists, philosophers, and scientists, such as Malthus, Hazlitt, and Davy. And we have been honored to dine with every major poet, Mr. Wordsworth and Mr. Coleridge included. From the intellectuals, I've heard fiery arguments about population control and why anarchism is preferable to democracy. On the other hand, the poets have ennobled my heart. I've been soothed by hearing Mr. Wordsworth read from his "Ode to Intimations of Immortality" and I've imagined my soul traveling to earth "trailing clouds of glory." I've also heard Mr. Coleridge's sonorous voice reciting his "Rime of the Ancient Mariner." I know that I should feel for the man who killed the albatross and that I should understand that all things are beauteous, even the snake, but the mariner gave me chills and nightmares and I wished that I had not heard Mr. Coleridge repeat his poem as the mariner does as his recompense for his great failings. Afterwards, I was so frightened that I crawled into bed with Miss Adela. Her zombie tales are not nearly as horrifying as Coleridge's Mariner's. I would rather have heard his "Christabel" in its entirety, but apparently he has not found a suitable ending for this poem. Such are the stumbling blocks to writing. But we all experienced terrified rapture, when we heard him proclaim and warn us of his vision in "Kubla Khan":

> A damsel with a dulcimer
> In a vision once I saw:
> It was an Abyssinian maid
> And on her dulcimer she played.

Singing of Mount Abora.
Could I revive within me
Her symphony and song,
To such delight 'twould win me,
That with music loud and long,
I would build that dome in air,
That sunny dome! Those caves of ice!
And all who heard should see them there,
And all should cry, Beware! Beware!
His flashing eyes, his floating hair!
Weave a circle round him thrice,
And close your eyes with holy dread
For he on honey-dew hath fed,
And drunk the milk of Paradise.

His "Kubla Khan" makes *me* "close my eyes with holy dread" and dream of other worlds, of paradise on earth itself, not in some far off afterlife.

1812

2 January 1812

Recently, the young poet Percy Bysshe Shelley joined the circle of friends. I find him truly intriguing with his comely looks, his quick wit, and brilliant mind. I was so taken with him that I wanted to know more about him. So, when Father was away at the British Library one afternoon, I stole into his study and perused some of the letters that Shelley and Father exchanged. Father had haphazardly left them atop his desk so I felt little guilt in reading them; they were out in the open for anyone to read who might be passing by. Initially, Mr. Shelley wrote a letter of introduction to my father from Dublin where he was writing pamphlets about Irish independence. He wrote a sort of "fan" letter where he confessed to my father his great admiration of Father's political philosophy located in his *Political Justice*. Mr. Shelley too believes that if all people exercised their reason, we would need no government. We would be free and would properly self-govern. He asked to become my father's adept for he wishes to learn all that he can from him. He solicited my father's guidance.

Father thanked him for the letter, espousing mutual admiration for Mr. Shelley's mind, but he warned him about his continued pamphleteering, which could lead to his arrest. He advised him to desist and that his actions were, even though based on noble intentions, "preparing a scene of blood," his own and others'. He reminded him what had happened in 1803 to Robert Emmet whom the British government ordered hanged, drawn, and quartered. Emmet was convicted of treason and hanged and then beheaded on Thomas St. in front of St. Catherine's in Dublin. Taking up arms against the British government in Ireland, especially since the penal laws were now in effect barring Irish Catholics from owning land, would not lead to lasting freedom or reform. Father advised Mr. Shelley to quickly return to London and that once home, he was most welcome to visit our home. Apparently, Mr. Shelley took this to heart and heeded Father's caveat because soon after he was back in London.

3 March 1812

Mr. Shelley came to dinner with his wife Harriet, a timid girl, slightly older than me. After dinner, when I inquired further about Mr. Shelley's life, Father told me that Mr. Shelley told him that he saved Harriet, one of his sisters' school friends, from her despotic father; Father confessed to me that he thought Mr. Shelley noble when he acted the hero and he eloped with Harriet to Scotland on a whim. Like my father, Mr. Shelley believes very much in female and male equality and will not abide tyranny.

Beyond his heroism, Mr. Shelley is also becoming known for his audacious broad-mindedness. He shared with the group his poem, "Queen Mab," which envisions the future and which postulates an infinity of worlds. It is rather heretical and he claims that if he had lived in an earlier era he may have been burned at the stake, as Giordano Bruno, the Dominican friar, was; Bruno, known as *Monsieur l'heretique* in the French Court, first glimpsed the infinite universe in 1600 and now Mr. Shelley has. To me he seems both prescient and omniscient. When I expressed this sentiment to Father, he laughed and told me not to worship a golden calf, even if he is a handsome, brilliant one.

Mr. Shelley dedicates the poem to his wife Harriet. He claims that her love "wards off the poisonous arrow of [the world's] scorn." It seems he believes that she is somehow his protector, rather than the other way around. Truly that accords her much credit and makes *her* heroic. He also attests that his character Ianthe in "Queen Mab," who meets and learns about the past, present, and future from the fairy queen, is based on Harriet. It becomes more obvious to me as I grow to maturity that one should not judge a person by first impressions. Surely there is more to Harriet than meets the eye, if my "golden calf" worships *her*.

And yet I am confused because Harriet's personality belies Mr. Shelley's valiant characterization of her; she seems so meek. I wonder how she proves to bolster him and keep him from ridicule and the world's scorn. After Mr. Shelley and his wife left, Fanny and I were in our bedroom. I was re-reading "Queen Mab" and Fanny was sewing a baby quilt that she was making for the poor house. I remarked that Harriet Shelley must be an extraordinary creature. Fanny agreed and suggested that perhaps she is like our mother, if the famous Mr. Shelley thinks so highly of her. Just then Mrs. Clairmont called for Fanny, probably to ask Fanny to comb out her hair. Or read the Bible to her. I returned to "Queen Mab" and tried to imagine Harriet Shelley as Ianthe, but I failed to see the resemblance. And even less so to our mother.

5 June 1812

This journal is not contiguous. There are times when I have not felt compelled to write in it, but now, I will reflect on my recent journey and about my mother's life, which I have pondered considerably of late. I often imagine speaking with my mother, whenever I sit by her grave. It is difficult to record those conversations. They engender such longing that I find it hard to write about them without weeping. So, I will speak first about my travels and then reflect on my mother's journeys and her life before she met my father, Godwin.

I recently returned from Scotland, where my father sent me for further education on my own. And to be fair, he wished to create distance between me and my fractious stepmother who was growing increasingly contemptuous of me. I was glad to get away from her and to head north to where the "barbarians" live. The Baxters, my father's friends and my hosts in Dundee and later in the Highlands, were certainly not "barbarians," but rather highly refined and generous people. Their daughters were my age and we quickly became friends. When I arrived, Mr. Baxter shared with me the letter that Father wrote him as I sailed, a letter which expresses great depth of feeling for my well-being and for his hopes for me. In it he writes:

> I cannot help feeling a thousand anxieties in parting with her, for the first time, for so great a distance, and these anxieties were increased by the manner of sending her, on board a ship, with not a single face around her that she had ever seen till that morning. She is four months short of fifteen years of age . . . I daresay she will arrive more dead than alive, as she is extremely subject to sea-sickness, and the voyage, not improbably, will last nearly a week.

And later, he weighs in on my character and his hopes for me,

> [Although] I am not a perfect judge of Mary's character, I believe she has nothing of what is commonly called vices, and that she has considerable talent. . . . I am anxious that she should be brought up like a philosopher. I should also observe that she has no love of dissipation, and will be perfectly satisfied with your woods and your mountains. . . .
>
> I am, my dear sir, with great regard, yours,
> William Godwin

So even though he provides Mr. Baxter with an assessment of my character and instructions about my care and how I should be "brought up like a philosopher," he was not overly cautious about my trip to Dundee. He sent me away on my own with only an acquaintance, Mrs. Nelson, as my guardian on the ship. Yet, this trip to Scotland was not in the least like the kind of excursion that my mother undertook by herself with my sister Fanny, when Fanny was a toddler. My father arranged all of the travel and living arrangements for me and I was comfortable and well-cared for. Even so, the journey has piqued my interests in travel and in exploring the world. Now that I've travelled north into the Highlands where the "barbarians" live I have the desire to see the far reaches of the earth, just like Milton's Eve.

I hope to visit France, Portugal, and Scandinavia, as my mother did, and tour the continent, just like young men are encouraged to do, and even travel to the Far East and India; "Kubla Khan" inspires me.

My mother traveled when she was slightly older than me. She visited Lisbon, Portugal, not for fancy or exploration, but to nurse her beloved Fanny Blood, who unfortunately had consumption and who was about to give birth. I wish that I could hear my own mother's words about the loss of her dearest friend. I have never had an intimate female friend. My sister Fanny and my stepsister Jane Clairmont, I suppose, are my closest female friends. Fanny is the dearest person with a warm, forgiving heart, but she is not interested, as Father and I are, in grand, radical ideas or literature so I find that Fanny and I have little in common. I do love her though, especially because she was our mother's love-child. On the other hand, Jane pretends to care about literature and philosophy, but her mind is not expansive and she can be petty and annoying, and like her mother, jealous of my father's affection. Neither of these relationships resemble the love that my mother had for Fanny Blood, whom she considered her superior in all things. Fanny wrote, sang, and drew better than my mother. Her brilliance surpassed my mother's at the time, but her excellence did not beget resentment but only pushed my mother to improve all aspects of her innate abilities. (Jane is not my superior; she is always seeking vain attention; she is so very much like her own mother, Mrs. Clairmont. And Fanny, the dear heart, always thinks of herself as inferior to me. She praises me, even when I don't deserve praise).

How broken-hearted my mother must have been when she held her Fanny in her arms as Fanny took her last breath. I cannot imagine the horror of witnessing one's beloved die and pass on into another world, never to see or hear from them again except in dreams. I fear that I would not survive such loss, but, as Father says, we must always prepare ourselves for tragedy, which, in some way or another, infects all of our lives. Regretfully, tragedy and suffering are surely part of the human condition. This is why the Greeks wrote their dramas, which remind us of the potential for and reality of tragedy and how we may purge ourselves of our anguish.

I have read with interest that my mother wrote "Thoughts on the Education of Daughters" as a way to financially assist Fanny Blood's parents in their return to Ireland, after their daughter died. The proceeds from the sale of her book went directly to Fanny's parents, which seems appropriate since my mother and Fanny developed their educational philosophy in concert. What a compassionate and generous heart my mother had! I only hope that my heart will grow in charity too. I must learn to forgive those people in my family who sometimes deliberately hurt me and I must always seek to empathize with the suffering of others.

16 July 1812

Not long after she helped Fanny's parents return to their homeland, Mother made her own journey to Ireland, her mother's home, taking the dreaded position as a governess, little more than a servant to the family of Lord Kingsborough. I assume that she hoped to exercise her philosophy about educating girls, but she most likely needed the work to support herself after the school that she ran with Fanny and her sister Eliza closed after two short years. My father wrote that Lady Kingsborough treated my mother with the usual disdain felt for governesses as did the girls in my mother's charge. They taunted and ridiculed "Mistress Mary," calling her "Mary, Mary, quite contrary." They believed that they were better than her because they possessed peerage titles. However, somehow, she eventually won over the eldest daughter, Margaret, who developed a great affinity for my mother and her love of thought, words, and writing. My mother encouraged Margaret to write, to think freely, to exercise her body, and to acquire the virtues that some men possess, especially fortitude. How fortunate Margaret was to have been tutored by my mother, a privilege I was never granted.

What was my mother's reward in mentoring young Margaret? Dismissal by Lady Kingsborough who was jealous of her daughter's abiding affection for my mother and who argued with my mother about the need for Margaret to become a lady and wear stays, to be confined to the cage of the whalebone corset, in order to be presented at Dublin Castle. I imagine that my mother audaciously challenged Lady Kingsborough and told her that a true lady is one who can be an equal companion to man, a woman who grows in intellect, reason, and wisdom, not some debutante to be presented at the King and Queen's Progress. Besides, I don't know that I would want to be presented to Mad King George for fear that his madness would somehow rub off. I've heard that even Queen Charlotte refuses to visit with him, worrying that his madness is as contagious and deadly as leprosy. Besides, in my view, Queen Charlotte would be far more exciting to meet; she is an amateur botanist who has been instrumental in the growth of Kew Gardens in London. I have also read that she is such a stupendous singer that she sang an aria with the young Wolfgang Mozart, when he visited London. She has also advocated on behalf of women's education. (Perhaps she read my mother's work. If I ever get a chance to meet her, I will ask). How much better off we would be if she were the Head of State and not our mad king who often babbles nonsense like a child and who has been known to foam at the mouth like a rabid dog! God save us from this mad monarch.

20 July 1812

One positive aspect of working for the Kingsboroughs is that she wrote her *Mary, A Fiction* during this period. It may not be the best of her writing. Even to my young eyes, it seems stilted and somewhat melodramatic, but, as my mother says in her preface, she disdained the usual sort of novel, which is given to romance and improbable plots; instead she says that it is not a novel. In actuality, it is a social critique of women's lives and their lack of freedom. It also critiques those, like the Kingsboroughs, who believe that their hereditary titles make them superior to all others; the Kingsboroughs' only aim in life was to dress well and have their supposed inferiors serve them by waiting on them hand and foot. Their only other concern was "What would the world think?" about whatever they said or did. They were only concerned with their status among their peers and counted that as the most important consideration. How awful to always fret about what others think! I give it little thought as did my mother. There is also much in this fiction that refers to my mother's travels but also her critique of marriage. Her character, Mary, looks forward to another world where there is "neither marrying nor the giving in marriage." I do understand the stance that my mother took; she believed that marriage was akin to slavery for women, a type of legal prostitution; yet, if true, why did she marry my father? Perhaps she agreed to marry Godwin only for my sake, so that I would not be labelled a bastard child and subsequently shunned by society, but also perhaps because her marriage, unlike most, was one of equals. She and my father even kept separate households, in order to maintain their independence. And these separate households, which were just blocks apart, allowed them not only independence, but the ability to send frequent and ardent love letters to one another.

I secretly nicked the key to my father's desk and read some of them. Once I counted over 100 letters that they wrote to each other. Most expressed deep and abiding love, but some were filled with anger and the passion that arises from misunderstanding. I was so moved by their content that I surreptitiously copied two letters that they exchanged after a quarrel on 17 August 1796. In her letter, my mother threatened to end their relationship. Apparently she was so hurt by whatever had passed between them that she wrote to him in the morning, "Could a wish have transported me to France or Italy, I should have caught up my Fanny and been off in a twinkle. . . . I can only say that you appear to me to have acted injudiciously; and that full of your own feelings . . . you forgot mine. . . . I am hurt—But I mean not to hurt you. . . . I will become again a *solitary traveler*." He responded quickly, early in the afternoon, "I longed inexpressibly to have you in my arms. Why did I not come to you? I am a fool. I know the acuteness of your feelings, and there is nothing upon earth that would give me so pungent a remorse, as to add to your unhappiness. Do not hate me. Indeed I do not deserve it. Do not cast me off. Do not again become a *solitary traveler*." How odd to hear my father practically beg Mother to continue to love him, to not abandon him, to remain his beloved, to not be a solitary traveler. Perhaps Mother's death snuffed out all such desperate longing. Yet his letters suggest how much he passionately loved her.

If I marry, I will follow my parents' example; I will marry for love and passion; I will marry my intellectual equal; I will not worry about what the world will think. Like my mother, I will endeavor to maintain independence in thought and action.

20 October 1812

1792 must have been a monumental year, both in my dear mother's life, but surely in the history of humanity. That was the year that her magnum opus, *A Vindication of the Rights of Woman* was published by Joseph Johnson, her mentor. 1792 was also a watershed year since it was four years after the storming of the Bastille and two years after my mother boldly confronted the famed Irish orator and polemicist Edmund Burke in her *A Vindication of the Rights of Man* about his inconsistencies in regard to revolution and his belief that traditions and hereditary honors must be maintained in order to preserve social and political stability. She and her liberal friends felt that Burke betrayed them. He had previously advocated for the abolition of slavery, the emancipation of the Irish, American independence, and the reform of parliament. Now, he presented rigid conservative views that upheld and maintained the supposed natural hierarchy. He worried that the revolution would spread to Britain and that the monarchy would be abolished.

In 1792, my mother traveled to Paris to witness the French Revolution and to dwell among the revolutionaries and the British ex-patriots who lived among them, including the writer and translator Helen Maria Williams who traveled alone to live in France during the revolution. They had dreamed of other "worlds" and all believed that a new world had been established and that people are born with rights, that one's "station" in life is not predicated on birth, and that all people are one another's equals. What an exciting time to be alive, when the princess and the pauper were now on equal footing! Humanity seemed capable of perfection and an ideal world was on the cusp of being created. My mother must have been truly enthralled to have entered that new world of limitless possibilities.

I've read though that this ideal world, this new heaven on earth, quickly became a literal hell. Mobs roamed the streets executing priests, aristocrats, and dissenters. They killed thousands, either by guillotine or hanging them from churches, colleges, and town halls. They tried them by mob rule, not in the court of law. Saints and sinners died alike.

Godwin describes a moment that was truly horrifying. My mother returned to Paris from visiting a friend in Provins and witnessed this mob rule; dissenters against such barbarity, whom she knew, including the leader of the Girondists, Jean-Pierre Brissot, who opposed the Jacobins and Robespierre, were executed in front of her; blood saturated the road as the mob shouted, "Hang them! Off with their heads!" When my mother cried out trying to save her friends, a female bystander, one of the sans-culottes, shouted her down and warned her to remain silent or she would be next. Oh, the horror and dismay she must have felt to have seen the great promise of the revolution and the rights of man turned into Dante's hell, where passion and barbarism prevailed!

The next year Louis and his wife were guillotined. I've not been to Versailles but I have heard of its great opulence, its galleries and ballrooms filled with gold and crystal chandeliers. And I am cognizant of Marie Antoinette's contempt for the hungry and poor, of her order, "Let them eat cake!" when she learned that there was no bread to be had. She lacked a soul in failing to recognize her obligation to other humans. Of course, here in England in 1649, the Parliamentarians executed Charles I in a similar way and tried to abolish the monarchy, but to no avail. The same situation has now occurred in France, because the once heroic Napoleon declared himself emperor and he still prevails in France, destroying the true sense of the original "rights of man." In some ways, I am glad that my mother did not witness the travesty that has occurred whereby one "king" supplanted another, all with the hope of creating true "equality."

1813

18 January 1813

I've now come to the portion of my mother's story about which it is exceedingly difficult to write; it is part of the forbidden knowledge, which my father wished to withhold from me. My father was honest in his memoir of her life, perhaps too honest, in revealing much of what transpired in Mother's life in 1795. The critic Robert Southey condemned this portion of the narrative and even wrote that, in blatantly revealing all aspects of my mother's life including her temporary despair, Father "had [figuratively] stripped his dead wife naked." I know that I've said that one should not care what the world thinks. Certainly my mother did not and yet I hesitate to speak frankly about my mother's love and lust for the despicable American, Gilbert Imlay, who impregnated and then betrayed her.

Because I am young, I have not known love between woman and man, but I have heard that love makes us blind. That the god Eros aims his arrow straight for the heart and that because of our love wound, we no longer think with our heads and use our reason but succumb to irrationality and passion. That must have been what my mother experienced. She was struck by that wicked arrow and lost her ability to reason! Her sense gave way to passion and obsession. She thought with her heart. I hope that this does not happen to me. I refuse to let passion dictate my life.

Perhaps in the beginning Imlay was good to her. Perhaps she thought that he was a fair substitute for her earlier, unrequited love; she had been attracted to a married man, Mr. Fuseli, the Swiss painter, and had written him many fervent love letters, letters that he refused to return to my mother and later refused to share with my father, (although he allowed him a quick glimpse of the letters and then abruptly shut the drawer), when Father asked to read them to prepare to pen Mother's memoir. I do not know her truest feelings about these men, because I do not have her words to tell me about her relationships with Mr. Fuseli and Mr. Imlay.

I know from my father that she claimed to be Imlay's wife at the American Embassy in Paris because, at the time, British people were in grave danger. 400 British citizens, including Helen Maria Williams and the American Thomas Paine, were imprisoned because the British and their allies took up arms against the French. At least Imlay cared for her to the extent that he was willing to pretend that she was his wife, in order to save her from incarceration and perhaps death. Indeed, she hoped to escape to America with Imlay and become his wife. They were engaged. Then she became pregnant and gave birth to Fanny.

That seemed to end the fledgling romance between her and the cad Imlay. He left my mother in Paris, traveled, didn't write to her, and eventually moved to London. My mother traipsed after him, refusing to realize that her ardor for him far exceeded his interest in her. When she arrived, she found that he had moved on and had taken another lover, an actress. Father says that Mother groveled in front of Imlay, begging him to love her as he once had. He did not consent to a sole relationship with her however. Instead, he suggested an arrangement, a ménage a trois. Apparently, she thought it over briefly but then did not consent, because she did not want to share Imlay with another woman and she had no desire to have intimate relations with an actress. So, as a consequence, he secured Mother a house in which to live. She continued to try to win Imlay's affection again. As I said, I've never been in love but I would hope that I would never grovel, when the one that I loved did not feel the same passion that I felt.

I try to empathize with my mother but her despair at the loss of Imlay was so deep that she tried twice to end her life. The second time she threw herself off Putney Bridge into the filthy Thames! How I wish that I never learned of her despair, the way that she felt unloved and rejected. It troubles my heart to learn that she wanted to end her own life because a man did not love her. It angers me to realize that the woman who a few years earlier boldly wrote about women's rights and sexual equality gave into such despondence. And all because of a man, an unworthy one at that.

I cannot comprehend her grief but am grateful that goodness prevailed and some kind soul fished her up out of that murky water so that she could live and restore herself to reason.

It seems that it took some time for her to finally see Imlay for the scoundrel that he, no doubt, is. At first he tried to reassure her that he cared for her but then she gave him an ultimatum. Ultimately, he told her that he did not want anything to do with her or his daughter Fanny and that he did not love either of them. She must have felt crushed. Yet she pulled herself out of her despondency and finally saw that he was not her equal in intellect, compassion, or generosity of heart. She broke with him in 1796 and, in that same year, renewed her acquaintance over tea with William Godwin. Thus, their love affair began.

Knowing her story, I too hope for a world where there is "neither marriage nor the giving in marriage," unless, of course, you have the chance to marry your equal, a fellow philosopher or artist with whom you share intellectual and physical passion.

1814

15 May 1814

Dwelling on my mother's attempted suicide was exceedingly painful. I now understand why my father viewed this as forbidden knowledge. I kept imagining her despair, her near death, and I dreamt of it at night. Sometimes, I even saw myself as a desperate soul jumping from Putney Bridge. I decided to bury this journal in my armoire until I no longer envisioned her despair. Now that it is spring and the daffodils are in bloom, I am no longer troubled by wild imaginings. I decided to revive my journal and begin again. Besides Percy Shelley has joined our "circle of friends" once more and his lively and brilliant presence, his passionate search for truth, inspire me.

Lately, Mr. Shelley dines with us almost every day. He remains captivated and aroused by my father's political writing and genius and aims to follow his anarchist philosophy. He has become one of Godwin's disciples. It seems to me, however, that Shelley has his own philosophy that guides him. He is considered notorious and his father reprimanded him because he was expelled from University College, Oxford, for refusing to deny that he and a fellow student, Thomas Jefferson Hogg, wrote a pamphlet entitled, "The Necessity of Atheism." Father says that Shelley and his friend based their conviction that "Every reflecting mind must allow that there is no proof of the existence of a Deity" on logical reasoning rather than the fallacy of an appeal to tradition or emotion. As Descartes attests, one only knows truth through one's senses and since no physical sense has seen or perceives a deity, it is logical, according to Shelley, that atheism is a necessity. I've not read the pamphlet but it must have taken substantial courage and independent thought to pen such writing, particularly since Oxford educates the clergy and has long been aligned with the Church of England. I only know this because my father explained these details to me about education at Oxford and Cambridge, places where someone like my mother (and myself) could have benefitted from an equal education. Alas, we are not men and thus do not have the privilege of an Oxbridge education. Perhaps one day soon this will change and women and girls will be allowed to enter the revered halls of these institutions. Perhaps one day we will outnumber the men who study there.

Even though Shelley has not admitted that he and Hogg wrote the pamphlet, their refusal to deny their authorship speaks volumes. If we can, at some time, speak privately, I will ask him directly about this pamphlet. He is five years older than me and his wisdom exceeds mine, although Father says that Shelley is prone to impetuosity and occasional moodiness. Such is the melancholic and mercurial temper of young genius. He's infected with the English malady! One expects this from such prodigious talent.

25 May 1814

I continue to read my mother's writings at her grave and, of late, have met Shelley there because he too wants to learn from my mother, not just Godwin. Fanny thinks that I am morbid and refuses to go with us but Jane accompanies us so that my reputation is not sullied. We often send her on a walk so that we can talk privately without her needless, inane interruptions.

Shelley thinks my mother brave that she advocated for free love and was perhaps willing to live with Imlay and his actress mistress in a *ménage a trois*. I did correct his misunderstanding. Nevertheless, Shelley thinks my mother bold, just like my father, and sees the same undercurrent of freethinking and breaking with tradition in my father's political writings. He also admires her advocacy of the poor Irish Catholics, something with which he has aligned himself. He favors Catholic Emancipation and, if he ever follows his father into parliament, he will be the Irish Catholics' champion. I greatly admire his ideals. He is so like my own father that he seems a younger version. Shelley is far more comely than my father though, whose receding hairline and sagging jaw mar his former good looks.

Shelley has recently confessed to me that he is separated from his wife Harriet. He has been disappointed in her mind, even though she attempts to improve it. I told him that I was surprised since he had dedicated "Queen Mab" to Harriet, where he seemingly professed his great admiration of her. He told me that this was merely wishful thinking. He had saved Harriet from her father and had hoped to cultivate Harriet's mind. Like Pygmalion and his Galatea, Shelley hoped to make Harriet conform to his vision of his ideal mate, a woman of intelligence, grace, good character, and beauty. Alas, he says that she does not possess those lofty attributes. He related, "Mary, she often reads banal writers. I had to beg her to read silently Mrs. Radcliffe's novels; I cannot bear to hear such rubbish." I was too embarrassed to confess to him that I have read and enjoyed *The Mysteries of Udolpho* and *The Italian*. Perhaps I will also write in the manner of Ann Radcliffe, what is being called Gothic fiction, which reveals much of what we fear that lies below the surface of our intellect.

It is unclear to me how anyone could possess every attribute that one would want in a mate. Despite his disdain for "Gothic" fiction, for which I can forgive him, I see in Shelley all that I would ever hope for. He may be capricious but his passion and brilliance excite me so that I sometimes cannot sleep for thinking of the possibility that I could be his ideal mate. I have not told him this for fear that I am not worthy of his affection. I think about him every minute of the day and dream of him at night. I think that I have suffered love's wound and that Shelley has taken possession of me.

Shelley and I have plans to continue to meet secretly and privately in Old Pancras Churchyard. I intend to sneak away at night when Jane is fast asleep. I don't want Jane as my shadow and chaperone and I fear that Father would not understand my meetings with Shelley, even though he greatly respects Shelley's poetry and his unconventional rhetoric and lifestyle. For now, all is innocent. Shelley is my ideal, but I fear that I am not his.

VINDICATED

15 June 1814

Tonight, I spent a good deal of time thinking about my love for Shelley, considering what my mother would say, if I could tell her that I am enthralled with him, that I too am in love with a married man, just as she was. My ghostly mother sat near her grave, unwinding her shroud, and listening patiently and carefully to my confession. She did not speak for the longest time, but then, pronounced that I have the right to make my own decisions and that I should, however, exercise caution with all affairs of the heart. "Do not let Eros blind you, love. Are you certain that the young man reciprocates your deep affection?"

I said that I didn't know, but that he kissed me gently on the cheek and gazed into my eyes; he called me his child of light.

She removed the binding from her hand and reached for mine. She entwined her fingers in mine. "That is a beautiful sentiment but you must be certain that he is a worthy mate for you, dear girl, and that he doesn't think of you as a mere child. You are a young woman with your own mind. Naturally, he is attractive to you because of his great soul but do not let passion drive your decisions. Know that your head must rule your heart in all things. I do not want you to suffer as I did, when I aligned myself with someone who was not my soul mate. But, if you truly love him with your head and your heart, then you should surely confess your longing for him."

I was grateful for her guidance and wished her a good sleep. She wished me the same and wound her shroud around herself again and returned to her grave. Even so, when I arrived home and climbed in my bed, I spent a sleepless night. I sat up all night gazing out the window looking for the stars but finding only darkness. Just before dawn, I heard a lark sing and realized that I must try to sleep. I laid my head down on my pillow but continued to worry that I would make the wrong decision and fretted that if I did confess my love, he would find me a foolish child, not his equal, that he would tell me that he does not feel the same longing. And, that, like my mother, I would be rejected in love.

Today a new world was born for me. Last evening, I wrote to Shelley and asked him to meet me at my mother's grave today— that I had something important to tell him. But before I could blurt out my love, he confessed his love for me and then I wept as I told him that I love him too. I love him with my head and my heart.

I have informed Shelley that today, June 27th, is his birthday. It is his birthday because today is the day that we made tender love on my mother's grave. Shelley was gentle with me and instructed me in the art of love. I know that this sounds blasphemous, but I can't help but think that my mother would be happy with my choice. Perhaps she even heard our mutual love cries and she felt happy about our union.

I feel ecstatic that I have found my ideal mate and that he finds me to be as pleasing as his highest ideal. I am his child of light and I feel that together we can be a formidable force for the good. We can inspire one another; we can continue my mother's and father's work and perhaps surpass what Wollstonecraft and Godwin accomplished. Our work can combine politics and beauty, can help humanity aspire to perfection, can breakdown old traditions and lead to a new, just world. One thing is certain. I will never let go of Shelley; he is mine; I am his. We are one. This is a true marriage of hearts, souls, and minds. I hope that my mother is pleased and that my father will find this a perfect union, similar to his union with my mother.

VINDICATED

My heart breaks; Godwin does not approve of my liaison with Shelley. Father learned (probably from Jane snitching on me to her mother) of our clandestine meetings and he forbids me from seeing my love. I told him that I consulted with my mother and that I will not give up Shelley, my natural mate, just as Mother was Father's ideal and perfect mate. Father told me that I am being absurd. He told me that I am too young to know genuine love; that I am still a child, and he insisted, "You cannot consult with your mother. She sleeps in her grave. Besides, you must realize that Shelley is a bit mad. And he's acting immorally. He has a wife and a young daughter or have you forgotten?"

I do not understand how Godwin, who sides with revolutionary thinking and who professes to believe in free love, does not understand my great affinity with Shelley. Harriet is not Shelley's ideal; she has failed to live up to what Shelley expected of her. Shelley even suspects that she has been unfaithful to him. I will not be unfaithful and I will live up to Shelley's expectations for me and have told father so. Surely, like Milton, Father believes in the right to annulment or even divorce when the two parties find that they are not suited for each other. I feel for Harriet and the child but Shelley does not love them as he loves me. Harriet is not his child of light.

I wonder what my mother would really think, if she were alive and not just my ghostly confidant. Would she bless or be opposed to my union with Shelley? I don't know but to be honest, she followed her passion and ended up deeply regretting following her heart and ignoring her head. Even if, as she was dying, she still felt love in her heart for him, she knew that Imlay was unworthy and ill-suited for her. Godwin was my mother's soul mate, not Imlay. And Shelley is mine. I tried to argue this point to my father but he was not persuaded. He seems to forget what love is because of his convenient marital arrangement with our former next-door-neighbor, Mrs. Clairmont—who is so unlike my mother that it is laughable. He should know that genuine love is an affair of the heart and head, otherwise, it is not love. He may love Mrs. Clairmont's body, but certainly not her mind.

I fear that Father may lock me in my room to keep me from my destiny. I will not be his prisoner but will exercise my individual freedom, a freedom for which he and my mother long advocated.

27 July 1814

Shelley forced his way into our home today. He pushed aside our maid and barged into the parlor. He told Mrs. Clairmont that he had to see me. She said that I was resting and not to be disturbed. She asked him to leave, but then he suddenly pulled out a pistol and put the gun up to his head, screaming "Mary, I need you." In the presence of Jane, Fanny, and Mrs. Clairmont, Shelley threatened to shoot himself, if I did not run away with him. Father heard the commotion and rushed in and shouted at Shelley that, if he didn't leave immediately, he would send for the constable.

I heard and saw all of this from the top of the stairs. I fear that my father is right, that Shelley is a tad mad, but what can I do? I adore him. I idolize him; I have no choice.

Later, when Fanny and I were alone, I told her that I feared that Shelley would harm himself, if I did not elope with him. Fanny tried to convince me that I was acting childishly, and that in the end I would regret my actions. Maybe so, I told her, but he needs me. I am his true wife, his child of light.

I knew that no one had ever held her close and whispered into her ear. How could she know how it felt to be loved? How could she know how it felt to be someone's ideal mate? How could she know what it felt like to have true affinity with someone? I felt sorry for poor Fanny but didn't say so.

I also felt a surge of love for her and, without thinking, urged her to come with me. But she declined, saying "My place is here with Father and Mamma; I am the eldest daughter and *they* need me."

I did not argue with her, because I knew that she was right.

She watched me as I quickly packed a satchel. Then I went straight to Jane's room. She was waiting for me with bag in hand. "He is terribly romantic, Mary," she said. "When do we leave?"

28 July 1814

Today, I broke out from my captivity. At dawn, I left a note for Fanny reminding her that I was Shelley's ideal, that he loved me and I him, and that she should not worry. Then, Jane and I stole out of the house and rendezvoused with Shelley in front of the Mermaid Pub on Fleet Street. Shelley had a carriage waiting for us, which took us to Dover. I was thrilled, but so nervous that I felt ill with fear. Even though it was early in the morning, I worried that one of my father's friends would see us with Shelley so I pulled my hood close around my head and Jane and I both wore face paint to disguise ourselves. I didn't care if the poison seeped into my blood or if I looked a zombie. Nothing was going to stop me from running away with my love.

We are making a tour of the continent, which is truly exciting. However, the crossing from Dover to Calais was exceedingly rough. Our boat's captain promised that the crossing would take only two hours, but a violent storm arose which tossed our vessel about. A squall nearly sank the boat as waves swamped it. I was terrified and clung to Shelley as lightning shot through the heavens and thunder roared above us. Eventually the storm subsided and the clouds dissipated revealing a blue sky, but being tossed about had made me gravely ill. I spent considerable time in the privy, while Shelley and Jane sat on the deck and continued to watch the waves batter the ship. I do wish that Shelley had stayed with me and held me close. A kind old woman helped in the privy and held my hair back when I became sick. She told me that such crossings are not bearable for many and that I should not be ashamed of my weak stomach. For a second, she seemed to resemble my dear mother, whose lock of auburn hair lies in the locket that I wear around my throat as a charm and remembrance.

Although I always suffer from sea-sickness, this physical disturbance was worse than anything that I have ever experienced. I do wonder why I was so ill while Jane withstood the storm and chortled in reaction to what appeared to be Shelley's amusing sea-faring tales.

2 August 1814

Once we reached Calais, we were delayed by the fact that somehow Jane's mother followed us and demanded that Jane return home to London. I felt sad, knowing that Fanny had probably betrayed us or that Father forced her to confess where we had gone. I was surprised to learn that Mrs. Clairmont didn't care that I had eloped with Shelley. Apparently, she was not speaking on my father's behalf, but purely on her own. She did say, with a good deal of satisfaction, that my father is appalled by my actions and that he no longer wishes to see me. He has disowned me. Her words shocked me and I wondered how he could react in such a wretched manner. He and my mother did not live conventional lives; they did not conform. I reminded myself of this and told myself that I can win back my father's affection once we return to England. After all, I am *his* love child.

After Shelley spoke privately with Jane, she told her mother that she is a free agent and that she would stay with Shelley (and me). I can only wonder what Shelley said to convince her and what her true motivation is. If this is my "honeymoon" tour, what can she gain from it? I don't relish having a jealous heart but Jane does spend too much time trying to beguile Shelley. She's a natural flirt and tries to capture every man's affection. It is obvious that she is half in love with him. I have nothing to fear though because Shelley chose and loves me; I am his ideal mate, not Jane, who does not possess any intellectual or creative acumen whatsoever. She is a replica of her mother, an empty but pretty shell.

Shelley and I have started a joint diary, but I will keep this one as well, in order to fully express my thoughts and record impressions and experiences. I have to retain my individual self despite my soul bond with Shelley. I must continue to own myself, as my mother advises.

I should note something truly bizarre that Mrs. Clairmont related to us. Someone is claiming that Godwin sold Jane and me to Shelley for £700 and £800 respectively! I know that Father has money problems but surely no one can possibly think that he would sell us like we are his horses, can they? We are not his property to sell nor does he believe us to be. How odd the rumor mill is. I am glad that we have fled stifling England for the continent and its freedoms.

10 August 1814

We arrived in Paris and have found accommodations that are quite meager, a small room at the top of the Hôtel de Vienne on rue de Malte. I find it charming, but Jane complains incessantly. I opened the window on the City of Lights and could see the Place de la Bastille in the distance. Shelley and I are eager to explore the city, but for now we are confined (like prisoners in the Bastille) not because we broke the law but because we do not possess letters of introduction and recommendation to accompany our passports. Shelley assures me that this will get sorted out but he also tells me that once we are able to move about the city that we must be frugal. Because his father does not approve of Shelley and his lifestyle, his father punishes him by withholding funds. Shelley has little in the way of silver for us, but expects to receive some soon through a very modest allowance and through a loan from his friend Thomas Peacock. In the meantime, we live on love, as long as Jane gives us the privacy that we need. I sometimes fear that she hopes to climb in bed with us. I also fear that Shelley would find that exciting and acceptable; after all he admired the idea of a threesome, but I have no wish to share my love with my stepsister who continually desires everything that I have. And I do not crave intimacy with Jane.

15 August 1814

Happily our letters of introduction and passports were sorted out so that we were free to explore the city. Today we visited Notre Dame de Paris and Le Louvre. We could only do so after Shelley sold his watch and chain that his father gave him when he left for Oxford. He briefly regretted selling them because they reminded him of a happier time with his father; however, it was necessary since the money that he expected to receive did not come through as promised. Shelley tells me not to fret about money. Ever since he was expelled from Oxford, he's always found a way to provide what he needs for himself, even when his father punishes him for not acting as the future baronet as he should. We don't abide by titles, especially now that we are in Paris, where titles and class distinctions have dissolved and rightly so.

The Louvre was extraordinary and Shelley and I admired Poussin's "Deluge," even as it horrifically portrays the Biblical flood. The painting was so realistic that we could almost see ourselves among the drowned and dying. One figure even looked like my Shelley. I noticed it first that and said, "Shelley, Poussin has captured your likeness," and Shelley remarked, "That is uncanny. Perhaps I lived in an earlier time."

Even so, we greatly preferred the non-Christian art. We relished observing the Greek statues, especially the Winged Victory of Samothrace and Aphrodite of Milos, better known as the Venus de Milo. Shelley served as my guide, teaching me about Greek form and how superior Greek sculpture is to anything that came before it. Overall, he seeks to understand how Greek art affected Greek literature. The community of artists, scholars, playwrights, and philosophers must have been astounding to behold. We hope someday to visit Athens and the Agora marketplace there in order to walk where Plato once walked and taught. We are, after all, not just Godwin's adepts, but we are also Plato's disciples.

Now, because of the art that inspires us, Shelley spends more time thinking about Hellenistic ideas, which he hopes to carry over into his writing. He is a true Renaissance man reviving Greek influence for our century. I intend to continue to study Greek so that I can participate in his intellectual activities but also to embolden my own intellect and writing. It is not lost to me that both my father and mother studied the Greek language. Father even made a daily two-hour habit of reading Greek and Latin classics. If I want to supersede their contributions to culture with Shelley, I must be as learned as my parents.

16 August 1814

We still have not received any funds and are essentially Parisian prisoners. Fortunately, there are no "Poor Law Bastilles" or work houses here and no creditors hunt for Shelley.

18 August 1814

Somehow Shelley procured a bag of silver, 60 pounds sterling, and we are now able to travel. We are on our way to Switzerland. He would not convey how he acquired the money, but he says that he came by it honestly. Perhaps Peacock came through with his loan, which Shelley will repay when he sells some of his poems. We have decided to walk to Switzerland, much to our hotelier's dismay, who warned us that there are dissolute soldiers wandering the countryside. She worried about our safety. We were not dissuaded. To help us carry our portmanteau, Shelley purchased an ass, which Jane and I take turns riding, with Shelley leading the creature, even though the poor beast has difficulty carrying one of us *and* our luggage. Jane insists that she should ride the beast more frequently than me, since she claims to be more delicate. She certainly affects more delicacy than me. Truly, she should read my mother's *Vindication*. I often suggest it, but she is not a scholar and has little interest in women's rights or fostering women's abilities. I don't mind walking, since walking builds strength and perseverance. The hills are sometimes difficult to traverse though and we have to rest frequently. I have felt ill of late, and have continued to feel queasy since the crossing, so Shelley refused Jane's monopoly of the ass. He told her to get down and let me ride.

If I were more of a believer, I would feel like we are akin to Mary and Joseph seeking a place to reside. Fortunately, we have not been turned away from the inn. Somehow, Shelley has sufficient funds to pay the proprietors.

We make our way to Switzerland at a snail's pace; I do hope we reach there before the snow covers the mountains passes.

Along the way, we have seen some appalling sights as we make our way through France. We witnessed burned-out villages, destitute and starving, gaunt people. The children were deformed, crippled, and diseased. Unfortunately, we had little to give them. They hungered for bread and stretched their hands out to us, imploring us for mercy, but all we could offer were a few napoleons.

We spent a wretched night sleeping on the ground because we failed to make it to our destination before night fell. Jane complained bitterly and claimed that rats were crawling all over her all night. I feared that there were bandits or unruly soldiers about but Shelley held me tightly, telling me that he would protect me from harm. I should not worry. That night I dreamt about the starving, dying children that we encountered. Their hollowed out faces looked cadaverous and I awoke with a fright.

We arrived at Gros Bois and had a delightful time resting in the shade of a large oak and eating our baguettes, cheese, and strawberries, and drinking Burgundy wine that we brought with us from Paris. The whole time Shelley and I said that we felt like Don Quixote and Sancho. Jane ignored us and droned on about her discomfort in Paris and the way that we neglected her. I was surprised that she didn't ask who Sancho was.

19 August 1814

Last evening, in Guignes, we slept in beds that were once used by Napoleon and his generals. We certainly are not trying to follow in Napoleon's footsteps, but one can't help it, since he laid siege to this land. Fortunately, Shelley doesn't in the least resemble the short emperor and he certainly has no imperial ambitions, but rather has anti-imperial ones.

Shelley admitted the folly of buying the ass; he thought it a romantic way to travel. Besides he sprained his ankle and could not lead the beast. He managed to easily sell the ass of whom I had grown fond. I named it George after Lord Byron whom Shelley sometimes labels an ass, even though he greatly esteems his work. George the ass is now owned by the hotelier in Basel. We now possess a hardy mule that carries our portmanteau and one of us easily.

23 August 1814

Shelley's ankle continues to distress him, so we sold the mule and spent several napoleons on a *voiture* and accompanying horses and driver. The driver, Charles Du Champs, is surly and rather odiferous and when we stopped for the night, the landlord insisted that he sleep in the same room with us. I was not pleased and neither was Jane, since Monsieur Du Champs leered at us and sometimes at Shelley. I had to place a pillow over my head because of his stench and his incessant snoring.

In the meantime, Shelley and I continue to read together, even during our sojourn through the Alps. We have read my mother's Mary: A Fiction; Shelley thinks it a flawed work yet delights in its overall critique of the aristocracy. He is not afraid to criticize himself and his own social class.

VINDICATED

29 August 1814

After a short stay in Geneva, we passed through the valley adjacent to Mont Blanc, the highest mountain in the range. Its magnificence astounds us. We have nothing like it in England or Scotland, where the fells present hiking challenges and great beauty but nothing as monumental as this. Of course, Scotland's landscape is in places mountainous but these mountains are unlike anything that I have ever seen or experienced. Mont Blanc juts into the heavens and the lower realms are covered in majestic forests of pines, oaks, and beeches. As we traveled, we heard a great rumbling and watched as snow fell in an enormous avalanche burying the glacier that lay at its base. Shelley quietly remarked, "This mountain is magnificent, like a great, breathing animal. It is best left undisturbed." We also heard wolves in the darkness. We were grateful that their howls seemed distant, although they may have been closer since we may only have heard the echoes of their cries off canyon walls. Fortunately, we observed no wolves or bears. Even so, Jane and I both huddled around Shelley in the night, as he kept his watch. All of us were frightened to hear the wolves bellowing in the night, but Shelley told us that we were safe. Our cabin was secure and he would always protect us. After a short time, I heard Jane gently snoring and I cuddled closer to Shelley whose body kept me warm.

Shelley has begun to take notes as he intends to write about Mont Blanc's terrifying and awe-inspiring sublimity. The gods, not just wolves and bears, surely dwell in its lofty peaks.

2 September 1814

We safely arrived in Lucerne, after spending the previous evening along the lake shore during a tempest. Winds battered the water and we had to seek shelter under the towering pines. Unfortunately, due to the inclement weather, Shelley has developed a hacking cough that worries me. We need to find a way to get to a warmer clime to help my dear Shelley. But I fear that this will not happen on this particular excursion.

We gladly parted ways with Monsieur Du Champs who was as eager to leave us as we were to be done with him. At one point, he nearly abandoned us, but luckily we caught up with him and we arrived at our destination.

After much searching, we rented two rooms in an utterly ugly house. The rooms are cold and inhospitable and we find it difficult to communicate with the Swiss because few of them speak French; instead they speak a corrupt version of German that we cannot comprehend. It was nearly impossible to obtain food and other necessities. Added to that is the burden of our precarious financial circumstances. We only possess £28 currently and have little hope of procuring more. Shelley has exhausted his requests for loans and gifts from friends. He must return to London to obtain more funds. After much discussion and contention, we decided that it is wise for all of us to do so. Thus our plans to complete our Grand Tour are unfortunately thwarted. The prodigals must return home. I wonder how we will be received.

Lake Lucerne is a glorious sight though. The town itself is nestled at the foot of the Alps, which surround it on all sides. We took a skiff when we searched for habitation. On the way, our guide told us to look up at the mountain that we were passing. "Do you see the snow on the highest peak? Once during a fearsome storm," he said, "a priest and his mistress, who were running away together, died in an avalanche when snow fell on them as they were crossing the peak. If you listen carefully, you can still hear their cries in the wind." Shelley scoffed but I was certain that I heard moaning and pleas for help. I moved closer to Shelley and threaded my arm through his. I vowed to stay clear of the mountains that are indifferent to human life and love. Indeed they are great, breathing (and sleeping) animals. It is best not to awaken them.

Despite our anxiety about finding lodgings and the strange feelings provoked by the terrible tale that we heard, I soon began to settle and after some time felt a sense of serenity as we glided along the placid waters. The mountains' reflection in the water added to this sublime experience. Like my mother, I am drawn to nature and find God present in it, even if that nature includes elements of terror. If it weren't for the inhospitable people who live in Lucerne, I would be happy to reside here with my Shelley, even though many of the inhabitants, including numerous members of the Swiss Guard, supported and fought for the French Royalty during the revolution. The natural environment bequeaths a certain sense of calm that I have rarely experienced. It reminds me very much of the romantic scenes that my mother describes in her travels in Scandinavia.

I wish that I could always carry that calm within me, especially when Shelley undergoes his occasional mania. Sometimes he stays up all night, pacing the room, fretting about a stanza. I prefer writing my poems in the light of day, when my mind is the sharpest and the images arise before me like vivid dreams. Yet, sometimes, my best ideas come to me just as I lay my head on the pillow and I am forced to arise and jot down those thoughts before they escape into the netherworld.

With little funds available, we decided that the least expensive way to return to England would be via a water route. We are travelling on the Rhine and regularly see medieval ruins with their turrets projecting into the heavens. Vineyards grace the prominences and we see workers tending row after row of grapevines that line the hills. Certainly, the scenes are picturesque. Last evening, we heard the vine dressers singing about shepherds and lost love. Despite such a bucolic and romantic scene, Shelley and I fretted very much about the workers and wonder how well they are paid. We fear that their lives are much like their medieval ancestors' lives.

En route to Strasburg, we were horrified to learn that a boat with 15 people aboard overturned and all of the souls perished. We saw the capsized boat as it drifted down stream and our boatmen crossed themselves to ward off evil. I was grateful that the water was calm and that we were not in danger of meeting the fate of those unfortunate souls. Nevertheless, when Shelley turned his head, I quickly crossed myself as well.

Regrettably, even though the waters were calm, Shelley had to come to my rescue on the boat by defending me from the brutalities of our fellow passengers, mean-spirited, barbaric men who were drunk and cruel, and who stole our seats when we had alighted for some refreshments. We could not understand their speech but found them to be exceedingly rude and obnoxious. Their actions were also lewd toward Jane and me and they taunted Shelley. I told Shelley to ignore them but he became enraged, shouted at the men and when one of the men pushed Shelley, Shelley struck him, knocking him to the ground. The captain intervened and quelled the violence. Fortunately, my dear Shelley was not injured.

Perhaps because I have led a sheltered life, I never knew that such barbaric men existed. Are they truly human? Aren't humans capable, as the philosopher Pico della Mirandola says, of imitating the angels? As he argues in his "Oration on the Dignity of Man," God the Father has "made you [man] neither of heavenly nor of earthly stuff, neither mortal nor immortal, so that with free choice and dignity, you may fashion yourself into whatever form you choose. To you is granted the power of degrading yourself into the lower forms of life, the beasts, and to you is granted the power, contained in your intellect and judgment, to be reborn into the higher forms, the divine." Why did these men seemingly choose to degrade themselves and renounce the divine spark that Pico claims, and which I believe, is inherent in all of us?

13 September 1814

As we neared England, a gale arose and threatened to subsume our craft. The rain poured down and the wind nearly toppled the boat. As the vessel rocked, Shelley tried to appease my fear by advising that I watch the porpoises that sported near the boat; they seemed to play in the waves, jumping over one another and frolicking, seeming to defy the tempest. Shelley was delighted, but I had a hard time concentrating on the playful porpoises. I tried to steady myself by keeping my eyes on the horizon looking for land. I was exceedingly relieved when we reached Gravesend and stepped off the boat onto the safety of the stable land.

We spent our second to last guinea on the boat and were astounded that three of us had managed to travel 800 miles on less than £30.

14 September 1814

We quickly proceeded on to London. Shelley is on a mission to obtain the money that we need. He has found through corresponding with Harriet while we were on the Continent that Harriet has taken her revenge on him by considerably dipping into his funds. Even now, as I write, Jane and I sit in the coach outside Harriet's residence (she has returned to living with her father and mother) as Shelley visits his wife in order to convince her to share what she has squirreled away, to give him his own money. He must obtain money or we will have nothing to pay our driver!

I feel sick at heart. We only just learned that Harriet is pregnant with her and Shelley's second child. I actually wonder if the child is indeed Shelley's but I dare not inquire about it at this time. Shelley would surely fly into a rage, even though he suspects her of infidelity!

I can only imagine their conversation and the hysterical nature of it. She is probably cursing Shelley for running away with me and ruining her life and her reputation, for betraying and abandoning her. He, no doubt, is trying his best to be the voice of reason and is attempting to subdue her wrath. Most likely, he has to tell her that they have no affinity, as he and I do, that he does not love her as he loves me. Yet, if he tells her the truth, she may withhold his own money from him. Oh, I wish that I could be a fly on the wall in that parlor and see how he treats her and whether he still holds some affection for her, especially now that she is once again with child. My Shelley is not heartless and cruel so he is perhaps softening his message to her and promising who knows what. I have to trust that all will turn out well and that Harriet will come to understand that destiny has brought Shelley and me together. She will need to step aside.

I endeavor to remain free of jealousy, but my stomach is in turmoil; I feel physically sick the longer he is with Harriet.

I try to pay attention as Jane babbles on about Lord Byron and how she longs to meet him. She sits in the carriage reading aloud portions of "Childe Harold's Pilgrimage," talking about the disillusioned, misanthropic youth whom she is certain she could satisfy. I care not. I wish that she would cease her droning on; I tune her out and wait patiently for my love to emerge from the flat. Here he comes! He is smiling. We are saved.

2 October 1814

Rumors still swirl around us. They are concerned with how Shelley was able to "secure" Jane and me. People continue to claim that Godwin sold us for a fortune. But Godwin has acquired no fortune. Even though he has broken my heart by disowning me and refusing to speak to us, he continually writes to Shelley begging us for money. We barely survive on what we have in our coffers and the debt collectors are seeking Shelley once again. He has told me that he needs to go into hiding until he can find a way to pay off some of his debts. He promises that he can see me on Sundays because on Sunday bailiffs are not permitted to arrest debtors. Every day that we are apart, he writes to me telling me how wretched and lonely he feels when he and I are separated; he longs for his child of light.

Even though we must part temporarily, I know from his letters and from the affection he expresses when we are re-united that Shelley loves me and I feel closer to him than ever before. He told me about his meeting with Harriet and how she begged him to return to her. He confessed his abiding love for me and told her that he was sorry that he had injured her. He must be true to his heart, even if it causes her great pain. She sobbed bitterly and ordered him to "Get out!" She even told him that she and her child would be better off dead. Shelley did not fall for her theatrics, which he says are much like Jane's exaggerations and hysterics. When he described the scene, I briefly flashed on the image of my mother begging Imlay and her later despondency, but I pushed the image from my mind. Surely, Harriet is not a foolish girl; she was just trying, as my mother did, to win back her lover's affection.

Despite this, she did relinquish funds to him because, by rights, they are his, just as she is his property, a custom and law that Shelley and I despise.

Of late, I have wished that Jane would move out and acquire her own life. We discussed this before Shelley went into hiding. I am often upset because Shelley and Jane spend so much time together late into the night. Shelley tells her witching and ghost stories and Jane deliberately becomes overwrought so that Shelley can comfort her. Shelley claims that it's just playacting and fun, but I know that Jane is exceedingly fond of my love and she would do anything to gain his genuine affection.

Despite our efforts to remain hidden, her mother found us once again and has threatened to place Jane in a convent! We cannot imagine Jane being restricted to such a prison. She lusts for life and the male sex in particular. When Mrs. Clairmont revealed her scheme, Jane just laughed and said that she was ridiculous —that, even if her mother managed to confine her, she would break out! She would scale the walls, if need be, or swim across a moat. She would free herself. I watched the drama unfold and said nothing. Secretly, I wished that Jane *would* be sequestered in a convent. I hate that she continues to seek attention from Shelley and even though he is not vain and won't succumb to her seduction, he does possess strong lusts and physical needs.

Nonetheless, now that Shelley and I are temporarily separated, I am less troubled by Jane's presence and sometimes find comfort in her company. I even listen more attentively as she hatches plots to meet Lord Byron, who is a likely substitute for my Shelley. Perhaps if she does meet the good Lord, she will stop trying to win Shelley's affection and we will be rid of her.

VINDICATED

15 October 1814

I have spent numerous hours walking up and down Fleet Street trying to catch a glimpse of Shelley. I fear that the more I walk alone, the more likely someone might think me a common woman, a tart, or that my identity will be discovered and then Shelley will be in jeopardy. Because of this, I've had to take Jane with me, as my shadow and "chaperone." I grow tired of the fact that her tentacles reach so deeply into our lives. When I do end up seeing Shelley, there she is, as always, accompanying us in our rendezvous. I sneak away sometimes and venture out on my own so that I can have private time with my love. He cautions me to be careful because I may be followed and then the creditors would know where to find him and could and would likely cart him away to the workhouse! This I cannot allow, so I go incognito; I paint my face like a zombie and don a veil so that it is unlikely that I will be recognized. There's a certain freedom in my disguise and Shelley finds it amusing to make love to a painted lady.

22 October 1814

I just learned that we are with child. That explains my continuing queasiness and my breast tenderness and dizziness. I have no one with whom I can confide or ask about female issues, except for Jane and she is little help, since she has never, to my knowledge, been pregnant. And even if I were on good terms with Mrs. Clairmont, I would not ask her advice about what to expect in pregnancy. If she did offer advice, she would probably try to fill me with dread, telling me that I will likely die just as my mother did. That's how much contempt she has for me.

I am happy to know though that Shelley is thrilled to learn of the pregnancy. We are to be a real family. He makes plans about our love child. I do hope that he is more excited about this child than the one that Harriet is carrying.

Even without Mrs. Clairmont's imagined advice, I have some trepidation about the pregnancy. Only because of what I know that can go wrong. I think about what happened to my mother and to her friend, Fanny Blood. How does one stop the inevitable complications? What if I should bleed to death like Fanny? What if my doctors are as incompetent as my mother's? Shelley tells me that I am being overly anxious; he assures me that all will be well and that I should not fret, but I have unquiet dreams about this pregnancy and this child. I've dreamt that the child is no bigger than a mustard seed and that I have to water it to make it grow, but that it refuses. I can only hope that the dream is biblical in nature and that in the end the mustard seed is a good, not a bad, omen. I must trust that all will turn out well, as Shelley promises.

In the meantime, I write stories of a philosophical nature and I continue to write poems. I've asked Shelley to read my Juvenilia and he says that he will but every time I suggest that he critique it he has some other pressing business or his own work to pursue. While we were traveling, he also failed to read my writing and much of it was left behind when Shelley said that we had to economize our luggage. He had promised to have it forwarded to our next destination, but it never arrived. Luckily, I kept my journal on my person so that this record could not be lost. Perhaps when we are re-united in the same house he will have greater freedom to peruse my writing.

27 October 1814

Shelley is furious with me! I pawned his microscope and now he refuses to speak with me. We needed the money and I was able to obtain five pounds sterling for it so he should be grateful that

I am contributing to our livelihood. He was exceedingly fond of that microscope though; it was his most treasured possession, and I didn't realize how much it meant to him and that his father had given it to him on his eighth birthday. He has peered at all sorts of animalcule and flies' wings under it. I did not know that he had possessed it for so very long and I feel a bit regretful, but we were desperate for money.

Shelley is also angry because he thinks I do not understand that he is not just a poet, but he is a natural philosopher interested in all things seen and unseen. He has a great fascination for electricity, mesmerism, and phrenology.

He even confessed that when he was young, he went to Highgate Cemetery and "chased ghosts." He visited graveyards at night, watching the "Resurrectionists," the grave robbers that snatched bodies from their crypts and sold them to doctors. Perhaps these are the gruesome stories that he shares with Jane that engender her hysterics. Although his "ghost chasing" sounds ghastly and could have easily resulted in his arrest, he learned much about human anatomy, when he occasionally followed the Resurrectionists when they delivered the bodies to doctors and then watched doctors dissect the corpses. Afterwards, he joined the gravediggers in the pub.

I do know about his fascination with science because I find him often looking to the heavens and here below examining ordinary objects, drops of water, insects, and other minute objects. I tell him that he is like Blake's woodcut rendering of Newton always gazing at whatever is in his close vision and whatever is augmented by modern instruments.

14 November 1814

Fortunately, Shelley and I are reconciled and re-united; he ceased being angry about the lost microscope. And, at last, our finances are improved. I don't know how he acquires silver because he does not share these details with me. Perhaps he borrowed more money from Thomas Peacock or Thomas Hogg. Sometimes when he does not share details with me, I feel as though he treats me like a child, as I feared he would, not his equal at all. I may be his "child of light" but I will not be treated as a child. I remind Shelley that I am quite grownup. I recently turned 17. I tell him that I am my mother's daughter and that I am strong and tenacious. He should not infantilize me.

Because I have been ill nearly every day with stomach ailments and dizziness, I have not been able to accompany Shelley on his jaunts about town now that he is a free man. Jane takes advantage of this situation and aspires to take my place on nearly every outing. I fear that Jane would like to permanently replace me. Jane and Shelley have traveled to the National Portrait Gallery to view the new portrait of Byron the celebrity and to St. Martin's in the Fields to hear chamber music from Handel. They stroll through Hyde Park's Kensington Gardens and reside next to the Serpentine Pond. Shelley tells me that there are lounge chairs that one can rent for a half-penny. Now that he is flush with funds, he and Jane rest there after their long rambles and watch the leaves turn orange, red, and russet, and fall to the ground. I beg him to let me go too but he tells me that the doctor advises that I rest so that I do not lose our child. I can feel the child stirring in my womb. She is as eager to get out in the world as I am.

Shelley's friend Thomas Hogg visits us frequently. He pays considerable attention to me and has even suggested that he and I have intimate relations. He confesses his love and lust for me. I find it amusing but know that, like Jane, Hogg wants everything that someone else possesses. If Shelley didn't desire me, Hogg would not want to bed me.

Shelley revealed to me that Hogg also tried to bed Harriet after she and Shelley were married. She refused him. I refuse him too because I only desire Shelley. Of late, he has avoided sexual congress with me because he fears that it will harm our child. Now, Hogg wants me to promise to join him in his bed. I know that they believe that free love is modern and that no one should "own" anyone else, but I cannot even think seriously about Hogg's proposal. I put him off and laugh at his propositions, telling him that perhaps after the child is born we can become closer, but I don't mean it. It feels like a game to me and that I am just a pawn in a game of sexual chess. I would rather be queen and move about as I like, making my own choices.

30 November 1814

Shelley received news that Harriet has given birth to a son. As soon as he heard, Shelley rushed to Harriet's side. They have named him Charles. I try my best to believe that Shelley will not return to Harriet but it is difficult when he expresses such affection for his son. And he often talks about his love for his daughter, Ianthe, named after his spirit character in "Queen Mab." I should be brave and gracious and remember that, even though I am Shelley's natural mate, Harriet remains his wife by law. She possesses his name, but I possess his heart.

1815

10 January 1815

We are financially saved! Shelley's grandfather has passed and has left Shelley £1000 per annum. 200 of that will go to Harriet and the children. Now I no longer need to continually fret that Shelley will have over-extended himself and we will have debt collectors banging at the door in the middle of the night or accosting Shelley on the street. In order to receive this annual allowance, Shelley had to forego ownership of a second estate valued at £140000. Shelley did not want to be a landowner and baronet anyway. We wish to live a simpler life. With these regular funds, we feel far more secure and can remain in our new lodgings at no. 26 Nelson Square.

Even in the cold weather I spend time in the glorious winter garden. I watch mothers and babies and dream about my child, imagining my mother sitting next to me advising me in regard to how to raise my daughter. I am certain that I carry a girl. I write stories about her and my mother and how they meet in a new Garden of Eden to discuss women's lives. My mother takes my girl by the hand and walks her into a new world. The world where there is neither marrying nor the giving in marriage.

My girl is quite the acrobat. I feel her tumble about within me, turning somersaults and doing the type of handstands that I've only seen court tumblers do. I do hope that when she is born that she will be able to participate in the kind of physical activity that boys often enjoy. My mother advocated such activity and advised her pupil Margaret King to play as boys do. Climb trees, run through the tall grass, swing the cricket bat, and enjoy the vigor of physical exercise. And Margaret King surely benefited from such physical activity, which also stimulated her mind. My father told me that she went on to become a revolutionary and a writer, just like my mother. I sense that my daughter will not be an ordinary child. She will be daring and will hang from her knees on tree limbs. She will be fearless and will be a new kind of woman.

I grow rotund and am eager for my child to be born, but I must wait patiently. She is not due to arrive until April when the daffodils bloom. It remains a damp and dark January. In late spring, I shall take her to a field of daffodils and read Wordsworth to her. Someday we shall travel north to the Lake District and visit Mr. Wordsworth himself and his sister Dorothy who is also a writer. We shall ramble the fells with them and perhaps Mr. Wordsworth will recite lines from his "Prelude" that recall his youth wandering those hills.

I intend for my child to meet with all of the poets, just as I did, because poetry and writing are in her blood. I am certain that poems and stories seep into her as Shelley and I write and as Shelley reads to me from his latest work. He writes about Mont Blanc and I continue to write my story "Hate," which considers human prejudice and its inherent evil. I ponder Hobbes's theory of innate human evil and juxtapose it with that of Rousseau. Are we born evil, as the Old Testament implies, or is it learned and acquired through society's corruption of us? What determines our ability to feel compassion and love one another? How much of this depends upon parental love? What would happen to an individual creature if they were utterly abandoned by its creator/father/mother? How would that creature fare? These are the things that I ponder as my daughter tumbles about begging to be let out of her confinement.

29 January 1815

I have felt well of late and so Shelley and I have spent our days escaping Jane, who now calls herself Claire, because she declares this name more "poetic" than plain Jane. Now, Shelley and I traverse London, walking from Trafalgar Square to Parliament and sometimes we take a carriage ride to Hampstead. We sometimes get disdainful looks because I am round with child and ought to be home and confined according to societal dictates. We ignore the hateful looks and I tell Shelley that the fresh air and my strolling are good for our child, whom we have tentatively named Sophia after Lady Philosophy in Boethius's *Consolation of Philosophy*. This name is fitting; perhaps she will become the philosopher that my father longed for me to be.

I do wish that Godwin would come around to meeting with me. I seek his forgiveness and love. I once worshipped him. Now that he has disowned me, I feel utterly rejected by my sole parent. I miss my conversations with him and his affection; we were so close when I was young. When I was a child, he read to me, took me to the pantomime theater, and played games with me in Regent's Park. He often told me that I was a duplicate, a smaller version of my mother, his love. And he treated me with the utmost affection. Yet, despite the fact that he has learned that I am with child, he still refuses to meet with me and Shelley and will only correspond with us through his solicitor, Mr. Higgins.

I find it troubling that he refuses to speak with us but that he still requests funds from us, especially now that he knows that Shelley has received his inheritance. This is highly hypocritical, but I suspect that Godwin's publishing business has not turned out as he had hoped. He would rather spend his days parsing and translating Plato and writing political tracts anyway. He has always been and will remain a contemporary Prospero. I guess that makes me his Miranda and Shelley his Ferdinand. However, these days Godwin labels Shelley a Caliban rather than Ferdinand; fortunately, my Shelley does not resemble the barbaric Caliban in the least, but he does curse as Caliban does, but with sibilant tones.

VINDICATED

Perhaps if our Sophia turns toward philosophy, Godwin will come around. She will be the ideal child that he longed for. I fear that I have disappointed him.

If that is the case, we have a long time to wait for Godwin's affection. Unless of course she is a genius child, which may be so, given her pedigree with Shelley as her father and Godwin and Mary Wollstonecraft as her grandparents.

2 February 1815

I have had vivid dreams that seem as real as the waking world. My Sophia stands at the door knocking, asking to be let in. For some reason, I do not respond but keep writing, even though I know that she wants to enter. I peer at her from the window, hiding behind the curtain, hoping that she doesn't see me. She is petite and her dark hair waves down her back to her waist. She persists and continues rapping at the door, but all I can think is "Not yet; do not come in yet. You must wait until you are fully grown and no longer a wee mite." I think this even though I see with my own eyes that she is not a wee thing but a child of seven or eight wearing a checkered purple and pink pinafore. I send my mother to the door to send her away but by the time she gets there, Sophia is gone. I do hope that she returns at the proper time.

Under my mother's guidance, I have been writing my child a story about a girl who refuses to wear a corset and foregoes the ringlets in her hair. She is as brave as any boy and is perhaps more studious. She does not play with dollhouses and dollies, but spends her time gazing at the stars at night, like any good philosopher, in order to plot their course through the heavens. She speaks many languages and travels to India and China; she rides through the forests on an ebony stallion, and braves the river rapids in an Indian canoe. Her name is Sophia and she is the girl of the future. She receives an equal education and can debate in grand halls. She's taken her father's place in parliament and votes with the Whigs for equal rights for all. She obtains women's suffrage. She is our Poet Laureate. She becomes the Prime Minister of England. When Sophia is older, I will give her this story. But I believe that she will live the story as I have dreamt it.

15 February 1815

It is mid-February and we have had a late snow, which is falling throughout London. It falls like French Lace to the ground and is quite exquisite to watch as it covers the withered rose garden. Shelley and I have hunkered down in our bed; we try to stay warm under the eiderdown quilt that I bought at a flea market. Shelley continues to work on "Mont Blanc" and he reads passages to me about the snowy peaks that poke the heavens and describes the thunder and lightning that strike the mountain's peak and illuminate the firmament. It's a fearsome and chilling sight. I ask him to stop and just hold me. He tells me that he will shortly but that he is working on a stanza in his head. So he has picked up his candle and has retreated into the parlor, telling me to sleep. Of late, he has not touched me for fear of harming Sophia. I tell him not to worry but he insists. I miss his tender touch and feel alone. I continue to ask him to read my writing, but he puts me off with promises of later, my darling.

I waited until I thought that he had completed his evening work and I met him in the parlor. I took his hand and we made quiet love on the rug in front of the roaring fire and then lay in each other's arms as the shadows flickered on the wall.

VINDICATED

This morning I awoke with cramping like a heavy monthly. I became frightened and went back to bed. I ordered Claire to fetch Mrs. Blenkinsop, who tended my mother in her confinement. She told me not to panic and advised that I drink liquids and lay on my side. I have done so, but the cramping continues to come and go like great waves. Tonight they have finally subsided and I feel comfortable. I feel Sophia kick against my hip bone and I know that she is all right. She pushes her little fingers up, which feels like she is in and of my ribs, which I know is impossible. I tell her, dear girl, stay in your cozy home awhile longer and grow to be a big girl who fills the space before you make your entrance into this world.

My mother visited me last night. I had just settled down to sleep and there she stood at the end of my bed. She was dressed all in white, her head covered with a hood. In one hand, she carried a book engraved with my initials. In the other, she pushed a baby pram. Was she suggesting I need to make a choice or was she assuring me that a mother can have a thoughtful, full life? That she does not intellectually and artistically die when she gives birth? I believe the latter. Mother believed that women are complete human beings who can be mothers and authors, mothers and teachers, mothers and members of parliament (if given the right to vote!). She lived her beliefs. As I started to speak, she walked away and disappeared like a mist. Perhaps the laudanum that I took for sleep conjured this apparent dream. I should perhaps forego taking the concoction tonight or maybe I will take it just so I can see my mother's face one more time.

The cramping returned more intensely last evening and within a few hours our fair Sophia was born. Mrs. Blenkinsop tried again to delay my child's arrival, this time by making me drink what seemed like a barrel of wine but to no avail. I feared for my life during the entire ordeal. I couldn't help but think of my mother and her friend Fanny and I seemed to see them standing at the end of the bed. I think Mrs. Blenkinsop felt their presence too. They were silent, but I worried that they would embrace me and take me with them. In retrospect, I should have looked to them for strength.

The pain began in my back and traveled around sharply to the front, all in waves that piled onto one another like a great torrent. There was much blood, which made me more fearful, but Mrs. Blenkinsop assured me that it was normal and that the child and I would survive. Claire stood looking horrified at the end of the bed, vowing that she would keep her legs closed or use one of those French letters so that she would never have a child. I told her, in between the pains that I would rather that she kept her thoughts to herself, although I also wondered how women have survived this unbearable pain century after century. I suppose it means that we are particularly strong; we are heroic. I doubt that many men could do as well.

Once it was all over, I held Sophia. Mrs. Blenkinsop looked relieved as the afterbirth passed intact. My mother and her dear Fanny Blood looked on and beamed at me.

Sophia is indeed a beautiful child with ivory skin and hair as dark as Shelley's. She opened her eyes and looked straight at me as if she knew me well. She responded to my voice. I held her next to my heart and she latched onto my breast quite easily without needing any guidance. Although she is tiny and arrived too early, she seems hardy. Mrs. Blenkinsop warmed bricks in the oven and she placed them in Sophia's cradle to keep her from freezing in this chilly weather. Shelley has been very attentive and he sang us both to sleep, singing a French lullaby.

28 February 1815

I am awestruck by this child who seems like a spirit straight out of one of Shelley's poems. I would call her Ianthe, but that is Harriet's daughter's name. Sophia suits my child. She snuggles next to me and her wee hand clings to my finger when she suckles. She seems quite robust for one so tiny. I would say that she's like a miniature doll but that would make her mere decoration which she is not. Her cry is vigorous and healthy and she lets me know when she is famished. Mrs. Blenkinsop has showed me how to get my child to feed when she is sleepy. She advised that I tickle her feet or express some milk with my hand and wipe it on her lips. She says that it is acceptable to nurse the child whenever she cries, particularly since she was born far too early, eight weeks early. We give her droppers of sugar water too, since my mother's milk does not yet flow steadily.

I feel some guilt that Shelley and I may have brought about Sophia's premature birth through our lovemaking, but I was cold and missed Shelley so and needed his touch. Her early birth seems not to have affected her health. She is as strong as I imagined her to be. One day, I shall see her hang from her knees on a tree and do cartwheels with Shelley in the garden.

3 March 1815

Sophia continues to thrive. Although only eleven days old, she is beginning to put on weight. Mrs. Blenkinsop told me that initially babies lose weight, but now that my milk has fully come in, Sophia's tiny cheeks have certainly filled out and her soft little belly begins to grow round. I do wake her occasionally to feed, because sometimes my breasts ache.

I sent word to Godwin that he has a granddaughter named Sophia, but have not received a response. Perhaps he is waiting to surprise us with a visit to see our baby philosopher.

6 March 1815

My heart is now shattered. I weep as I write in this journal; the pages are stained with my tears. I went to my Sophia's cradle this morning because I had not heard her cry out for me as she usually does when she is famished. I looked into her bed and she was pale and cold. I picked her up and held her close but she was as limp as a ragdoll. I screamed for Shelley who came running, but neither of us were able to rouse her. The life, the spirit fled from her. We did everything that we could to revive her. I opened her mouth and blew breath into her lungs. Shelley even slapped her back, thinking that this would cause her to gasp, but nothing worked. I screamed so loudly that the neighbors came running into our flat and they watched as I fell to my knees in utter despair. Shelley ran for Mrs. Blenkinsop and the apothecary down the street, but neither were able to bring her back. Mrs. Blenkinsop held me in her arms, as I sobbed. She acted the mother to me, knowing that my own mother could not embrace me.

Our fair Sophia is gone. We could not call her back from the other side; we could not resurrect her.

I am numb and feel hysterical. Mrs. Blenkinsop continues to hold me close as I rock our dead child. How could this have happened? She was well when I placed her in her crib and tucked her in to keep her warm. I tell Mrs. Blenkinsop that I should have kept Sophia next to me rather than leave her alone in her crib. I hope that she did not feel as though I had abandoned her. Mrs. Blenkinsop assures me that Sophia's death is not my fault. I cannot be consoled. She tells me to go ahead and weep; the tears will soothe my heart.

With the loss of my Sophia, so many questions trouble my mind: Where does the spirit go? What animates us and gives us life to begin with? I am reminded of my mother's words: "Life, what art thou? Where goes the breath? This I, so much alive." If only I could bring Sophia back. I would do anything to warm her cold body and re-invigorate her.

I find it hard to sleep and when I do finally meet the God Morpheus, I dream about Sophia who is always out of reach. Perhaps I am Niobe being punished for her arrogance. The gods have taken my child from me.

15 March 1815

Last night I dreamt of Sophia and that she had returned to life. Shelley and I rubbed her by the fire and she lived. She nursed and emptied my aching breasts. I held her close, vowing that I would never leave her alone again.

I awoke and found no baby.

20 March 1815

Thomas Hogg still believes I should be his lover. Unfortunately, Shelley thinks that I should be shared as a "treasure." I cannot contemplate such an encounter, especially while I am still in deep mourning and think only of my sweet child. We only recently buried her. The box was so tiny it seemed fit for a doll.

I am a treasure, but I give myself to whom I please, not as someone's bartered "prize." I own myself. Why does Shelley not understand this and why is he not as grief-stricken as I am? Perhaps it's because he already has two children. I have none.

14 April 1815

I continue to mourn and wonder if we are in any way responsible for Sophia's death. Shelley refutes this and says that he and Harriet often made love in late pregnancy. This does not help my grief but only adds to it. He tells me that it is best to bury my grief. I cannot. I wear black, even though the daffodils and tulips grace the woodlands. I dream of how I had planned to share all of this with my darling girl. Now, I dare not sit in the woods and the fair face of the daffodil brings me no solace, only a deep desire for my child who sleeps below the ground tucked in next to my mother.

Sometimes I think that I hear Sophia cry out in the night and I scramble from my bed in great haste to see if she is in her cradle. But no. The cradle is cold and desolate of life. If only I could bring her back. From where does life truly emanate? If there is a creator, is the creator cruel and reckless? Neglectful of our personhood?

A child is the father (or mother) to man (or woman) as Wordsworth attests. I wish I could believe as he does that we are immortal beings. If I did, I would believe that Sophia dances in a heaven full of wildflowers, bryony, and daffodils and that she waits for me and Shelley to join her in the dance someday.

8 June 1815

I pour myself into my work to combat my grief. I think constantly about metamorphoses. All of life is change, transformation.

Perhaps death is not annihilation but mere transformation. "Those are pearls that were his eyes. . ." as Ariel attests.

I think about the origins of being. What if a being were created that could not change? Or never grow old and die? What if they had the ability to learn great things and challenge themselves to ponder the thorniest of questions without fretting about paradox?

With the loss of Sophia and all the wisdom that is inherent in her name, I now assume her place as a philosopher and ponder these paradoxes. I dream about a new being who can withstand all adversity and trials, a being that could, through human contrivance, become transcendent of human failings and suffering. What would that being look like and who would dare create, incubate, and give birth to it? I talk about these ideas with Shelley who also dreams of other worlds; he defies the gods and the angels in whom he disbelieves. Such talk brings momentary peace and then I remember my sweet Sophia's face and my heart aches.

20 June 1815

I now feel free to sit alone in Hyde Park next to the serene Serpentine Pond. I watch children launch their homemade sailboats and couples lounge in their rowboats enjoying the sun as I write in my journal. I have seen Harriet, Ianthe, and Charles here enjoying the sunshine and the warm breeze, but I do not interact with her or them. She ignores me. I endeavor to feel the joy and enthusiasm that they feel at this moment, but I cannot. My head is filled with the darkest thoughts but also the more hopeful philosophical questions that guide my belief that someday humans can and will overcome death.

23 July 1815

I have wondered why I have felt ill of late. It appears that I am pregnant again and have been for three months. Naturally, I continue to wear black, as is customary for a year of mourning, but this seems foreboding during pregnancy. However, I must don my black gown and veil until I no longer grieve for my baby girl.

I find it difficult to accept this pregnancy because of my fear of losing this child too. I shall not name her or him. I shall wait patiently to see if this new life flourishes and sustains itself. In the meantime, I will work, and try not to lament every minute the loss of darling Sophia.

6 August 1815

Shelley has agreed to send Claire away for a time so that we can set up our own home at Bishopsgate. She will stay with her aunt in Scotland. She was angry and felt rejected; she claimed that we were banishing her to where the barbarians live. She lashed out at me, but Shelley told her that it was his idea and that it was for the best. She needs to acquire her own life. When he said that, she slammed the door on him and told him to "Go to Hades, where you belong!"

I feel such relief that Claire will not be in constant attendance and that Shelley and I can grow closer without her incessant interference.

15 August 1815

Shelley continues to be fascinated by natural philosophy. He has witnessed the invisible forces that surround us. At Eton, he regularly conducted experiments with electricity and devised a way to electrify the door handle to his room, so that the older boys who taunted him would get shocked if they tried to enter his cell. And he told me that when he was at Oxford he purchased an electrical, galvanic machine. He went so far as to attach himself to the machine and much to his and Thomas Hogg's surprise, Shelley's wild locks stood on end and bristled with energy. Hogg quickly turned off the machine before poor Shelley's brain was fried! Shelley says that he submitted to his impulse because he wanted to experience the effects of electricity. No sane person would undergo electrification, if they could help it! I hope that he's just highly eccentric and not a mad man.

Of late, Shelley and I have attended galvanic experiments at the University of London. They reminded me of somewhat similar experiments with electricity that Humphry Davy undertook with chemical elements and described to my father and his friends when I was a child. At the University of London, the natural philosophers proposed to animate a dead frog by attaching an electrical wire to the frog's appendage. Before doing so, the chief researcher asked an audience member (of course all men except for me) to approach and verify that the creature was certifiably dead. I quickly raised my hand and came forward. Naturally, frogs are cold and slimy to begin with but this was not merely cold and wet but hard like stone. The chief inquisitor, Mr. Cyrus McNabb, asked, "Miss, can you verify that the creature does not possess life?"

"Indeed, sir, there is no sign of life in the pitiful creature," I replied.

"Thank you, you may return to your seat. Now, everyone please watch closely and you'll witness something extraordinary, a resurrection of sorts."

He held up an electrical wire, switched it on, and it bristled with energy. It shot sparks and wriggled like a serpent. He then attached it to the creature's leg and within seconds the leg gyrated and danced with electrical impulse. The audience gasped and

Mr. McNabb turned off the current and the creature lay still. He repeated the animation and again the audience gasped and then cheered. The only problem seemed to be the inability to animate the entire corpse, which did not appear affected by the electrical current. Mr. McNabb said that soon they will be able to animate all of the protoplasm in this creature and others. It was no miracle, only the natural wonder of harnessing the energy of the fourth dimension.

I was excited by the implications of the experiment and I began to ponder the profound potential of electricity if correctly applied. What if it were possible to restore life to a dead creature via electricity? What a boon that would be to grieving parents, like myself, or to spouses whose beloved has passed into another world! Could you recall them from that other side merely by capturing and utilizing the invisible power all around us, found in what Mr. McNabb called the fourth dimension?

7 October 1815

I regularly attend the galvanic demonstrations and have even gone so far as to question the good scientists. I've asked questions that I contemplate about restoring life. They have affirmed that restoring life is ultimately their motivation; they too are curious about electrical systems within the human body. I have also asked them whether they think that the human soul is hard-wired in such a way. If you re-animate a body, can you animate a soul? Is the soul mere consciousness or something else? If a doctor could create a creature and thus play like God, would they imbue their creature with spirit and soul merely by using the electrical force found in nature or would some other act need to be performed? No one can answer these questions and sometimes they seem perplexed and troubled about why I even dare to ask. I suspect that some of them do not believe that we possess souls. Or perhaps they think it blasphemous to assume that a researcher might attempt to create life from scratch.

20 November 1815

I've read Hesiod of late to remind myself of Prometheus and how he displeased the gods by stealing fire from them and giving it to humans. The gods punished him for his transgressive act by chaining him to a rock and then they enticed a vulture to eat his liver. And each day the liver grew back and the vulture ate it again. Prometheus, the creator and benefactor of man, is perennially punished by Zeus for giving us knowledge. Certainly the gods forbid knowledge but why? And why do we humans seem to have innate curiosity about the unknown and forbidden? Are we all Promethean when we defy our gods and act in ways that we believe will benefit and improve humanity? If our Creator gave us the ability to create tools by which we can extend our senses and capabilities, is it wrong to use them to try to better ourselves and all of humanity? Are we to have faith alone, as Orpheus was advised to do, and not rely on our senses to understand and perhaps improve the world? Do we risk losing all our Eurydices by extending our senses and abilities?

I still dream of Sophia, even as the new child kicks and squirms inside of me, and I wish that I could use natural or even unnatural forces to bring Sophia back to me. I'd be willing to make a pact with Beelzebub himself, if such a being exists. Perhaps in the future someone will devise a way to restore spirit and life in a dead body. If that were the case, I would even resort to unearthing my child from her grave; I'd be like Shelley and become a Resurrectionist, so that Sophia could live and dwell amongst us and not in some obscure and unknown bardo.

Claire has returned from her exile. She despised Scotland and did not get on with her aunt who criticized her unladylike behavior. She begged Shelley to allow her to return. He gave in when she promised to find some occupation to fill her days so that she has her own life. To our amusement, she has taken up singing.

She is still annoying but she seems to have given up on trying to entice Shelley. Now she wishes to avail herself of meeting George Gordon, Lord Byron. She is sure that she can restore Childe Harold to life and ease his melancholy. She is arranging a rendezvous but also a plan whereby Shelley and Byron can become acquainted. Perhaps she envisions a threesome.

I read Byron's poetry and find it so very dissimilar to my love's poetry, which strives to imagine a more perfect world and a more perfect human. Shelley possesses high ideals, which he hopes to impart to his readers, whereas Lord Byron verges on intellectual cynicism; he's even an advocate for Bonaparte despite Bony's imperial tendencies. I favor my love's vision of the world over the skeptical cosmopolitanism that Lord Byron seems to espouse. Although to be fair, he also favors human freedom and fights for the underdog. He aligns himself with the Greeks who struggle for independence from the Ottoman Empire. He's a Panhellenist, because he supports the political union of Greek people, although I would not ascribe Hellenistic thought to him; he is no disciple of Plato as Shelley is.

I shall try more frequently to write in this journal. It offers me a way to ponder the grandest and most paradoxical questions.

1816

10 January 1816

This evening at dinner Claire said that she tracked down Byron at the Drury Theatre. She will pretend to be an actress in order to gain his attention. She will audition for Ophelia while he plays Hamlet. I would say that she's a fair actress, since she is often given to theatrics and hysterics. Too bad Byron can't send her to a nunnery.

13 January 1816

Claire has returned from her quest to capture Lord Byron. She announced to Shelley and me that as "Ophelia" she easily seduced Byron. He was her prey, she said. I find it doubtful that Byron was her victim. She thinks so much of her beguiling ways. Since she was unable to keep her legs closed, I do hope that she used a French letter as she had advocated. Byron is a notorious libertine. Claire risks pregnancy but also disease because the good Lord is not known for his pristine hygiene. Shelley insinuates that Byron has been dosed with mercury on many an occasion. I dare not tell Claire about this or that there are rumors that Byron and his half-sister Augusta have been sexually intimate; he has carnal knowledge of her and has even said that he is deeply in love with her as she is with him. Such rumors forced Byron to temporarily exile himself. And his wife, Annabelle Millbanke, is now seeking a divorce. Claire usually doesn't fear scandal but that would perhaps be too much, even for her.

Claire did add that for all of his boasting he is not a great lover, only mediocre. Plus, he has a clubfoot, which he tries to hide. She found him less than his manly persona embodied in his poetry. I, for one, feel sorry for his deformity. Even a lord can be belittled for his hideous imperfection and one must have compassion for those who lack complete grace. I have learned some lessons from Coleridge.

Perhaps Claire's ridicule of Byron is just her way of avoiding rejection; if she rejects him, his scorn for her will be less troubling to her and will help her save face.

24 January 1816

I have done my best to shield myself from the fact that I was carrying a child. I did not want to name her or him or to dream of the child as I did with fair Sophia. I may have inadvertently cursed myself by longing too much for that dear child. This time I pretended that I had just grown matronly and fat and I ignored the child's movements within, preferring to think of the movement as gas rumblings or a bad turnip causing intestinal distress.

But today, I could no longer ignore the biological circumstances. A boy child issued forth from my body after I suffered a great deal of pain. Mrs. Blenkinsop dosed me heavily with laudanum to ease the terror and after fifteen hours the child was born. Shelley never left my side this time.

The boy is a sanguine child, rosy-cheeked and comely. I held him close and refused to let Mrs. Blenkinsop take him away to bathe him. I fretted that Sophia died because I did not hold her close; now, I know that by keeping him near my heart, he will be safe from all harm.

We have not named him, but I told Shelley that I would like to name him after my father. This may bring Godwin around to caring for me again and perhaps he will forgive Shelley for seizing his only daughter. William is a good name, regardless of whether the boy is named for my father. He looks like a William; perhaps we'll call him Will and let on that he is named for the Bard or William Blake, rather than Godwin. Shelley affectionately calls him Willmouse and I concede that this is a good moniker for him.

10 February 1816

Shelley chastises me for refusing to let Willmouse out of my sight. The child shares our bed, even though the doctors and Mrs. Blenkinsop say that we mustn't sleep with the child. We could accidentally smother him. I am constantly aware of his presence in our bed and know that I would never roll onto him by accident. I am his protector. I keep him near my heart. My grave error with Sophia was placing her in her own cradle too far away from me and my heart and warmth. If I awaken and fear that Will is not breathing, I can easily place my hand on his chest and feel it raise and lower. This keeps me calm and content.

Shelley must be patient with me because I cannot bear the thought of losing another child. He tells me not to worry, that Will is a hardy child and will not end up in the narrow grave like Sophia. I recall Shelley's promises that all would go well with Sophia and remind him of that. Despite this, Shelley keeps assuring me that Will shall prosper. Shelley pronounces this so blithely that I think that this must be easy for him. After all, he already has two other children with Harriet. All I have is Will who is my only living love child.

Despite our attempts to placate my father and to pay tribute to him by naming our child after him, Godwin still refuses to see or to forgive us. He continues to disavow me. Shelley is beside himself with anger towards Godwin. He finds him completely unreasonable, especially since we financially support Godwin whenever we can spare the silver.

Godwin's ill will toward us injures Shelley profoundly. He was one of my father's faithful disciples; Godwin was his God incarnate. Shelley deeply admired him and his intellect. He believed in his politics and Godwin's anarchism that relies upon human reason. Like me, Shelley feels abandoned and betrayed by his mentor, his partial "creator." Ironically, because of this, he sometimes lashes out at me, not physically, but emotionally, saying that I am as cold as my ill-tempered father. That I have no real passion. That I have no true sense of love or duty. I defend myself and remind Shelley that nothing he says to try to belittle me has any effect; his cruelty towards me cannot affect my person. I still own myself, as my mother advocated.

Shelley is a bit mad; I knew this from the outset, when he threatened to kill himself. Even so I must forgive him for his anger. I know that he is not truly angry with me but with the man who rejects his creation.

As I feared, Claire did not use a prophylactic. She is pregnant with Lord Byron's child. She wrote to him, but his only response is that he is leaving for Switzerland. The child is her responsibility, not his. He's not even sure that the child is his. Claire is livid. When she read his missive, she grabbed "Childe Harold" and threw the book at the mirror in the parlor; shards of glass littered the side table and fell on the floor. Then, she ran to Shelley and wept in his arms.

Claire wanted fame and fortune, but I fear that her only fame is that she will be viewed as one of Byron's rejected tarts. She'll be another Caroline Lamb, Lord Melbourne's wife, although, unlike Caroline Lamb, Claire is not a Lady. Claire should have listened to Caroline though when she announced that Byron is mad, bad, and dangerous to know. And, I would add, amoral and immoral. He is a licentious libertine with a hollow heart who lusts after all that is forbidden.

Unfortunately, Claire has learned this the hard way. Somehow, perhaps through her mother, who is ashamed about Claire's pregnancy, she has heard about the rumors swirling around concerning Byron and his half-sister Augusta. Claire is disgusted. Plus, he is deeply in debt. He is now known as a Don Juan, but an incestuous, distasteful one.

1 May 1816

As I expected, Claire has quickly gotten over her disgust with the good Lord. And now that she knows that his wife has left him, Claire believes and hopes that she can replace her. So when we received an invitation to stay with Lord Byron in Geneva this summer, Claire beseeched Shelley to accept the invitation and to allow her to accompany us. Once more, Shelley gave into her demands and now she is ecstatic and holds out hope that she and Byron will marry and thus give their child a reputable name. I, for one, am not at all certain that this is Byron's hope or motivation to invite us to sojourn with him. His object of fascination is Shelley, for he and Shelley have been corresponding, sharing drafts of poems, and discussing politics and philosophy. I glanced at some of these letters that Shelley had on his desk and they make no mention of Claire's condition. Byron may not even know that she clings to us like a parasite. We cannot rid ourselves of her and, when we travel to Geneva, she will continue to attach herself to us, barnacle that she is.

It disappoints me that Shelley has not asked me whether I care to spend the summer with Byron. Of course, I wish to spend time in Geneva, and I believe that it will do Shelley good as he continues his projects, especially his sequel to Aeschylus's *Prometheus Bound*, but I do hope that we secure a private home. I do not wish to share lodgings with Byron. I believe that he is madder than my own Shelley, if that is possible. His madness could very well be a result of latent syphilis. And I don't wish Willmouse to be prey to Lord Byron's influence; Will is so very young and we are a new family. However, I have not shared these thoughts with Shelley who is as thrilled as Claire is about the prospect for a brilliant summer in Switzerland, where he can use Byron as a reader and critic of his work and thus continue his growth as a poet. I do not wish to dampen his enthusiasm, but I fear that Byron and I will not get on.

14 May 1816

After another arduous journey over sea and land, we finally arrived in Geneva. Traveling by sea was just as grueling for me as last time, even though this time I wasn't pregnant. As my father attested when I was young, I easily succumb to sea-sickness. Clearly, I lack the sea legs that Shelley possesses. Perhaps he was born of the sea, is composed of water, and I was born of the earth and am made of clay? Claire also took the brunt of the sea voyage well despite her pregnancy and the fact that the weather was consistently rough, more like a blustery fall than the calm summer solstice. The boat bandied about like a toy ship. But only

Shelley was able to sit on the deck and enjoy the voyage. He is a natural sea-farer and relishes the strong currents and rollicking waves. Surely, his mythical father is Neptune.

Our excursion through the Alps was also harrowing. I had never seen such desolation even though it is summer. Winter never seems to depart the landscape and the cold, damp weather makes everything feel foreboding. I felt quite relieved to finally arrive in Geneva. Even though it continues to rain, I have taken pleasure in watching the sailboats with their billowing white masts on the lake. I hope that the weather abates and that we can spend time sailing with Willmouse. Perhaps Willmouse will become a mariner like his father, but hopefully not akin to the Ancient Mariner.

1 June 1816

Lord Byron has finally arrived at the hotel, showing up in a grand Napoleonic carriage at midnight after visiting Waterloo to contemplate the battlefield. His private physician and close friend, John Polidori, accompanies him. Byron proudly announced that he has secured lodgings at Villa Diodati; he takes great pleasure in knowing that John Milton once briefly lived in this villa. I suppose he thinks that he is the reincarnation of Milton. But, I reckon that he is closer to Milton's Satan than to Milton himself. I wonder if, like Milton's Satan, he can make a heaven of hell, a hell of heaven. I doubt that he's that talented. But, like Milton's Satan, he does create Pandemonium.

The villa certainly is magnificent. It sits high on a hill over-looking Lake Geneva and is surrounded by bountiful gardens filled with roses, lilies, cuckoo flowers, and edelweiss. The villa itself is enormous and contains ballrooms, sitting rooms, open verandas; it presides like a palace over the lake.

I am grateful that Byron helped secure a private cottage for us. Once he heard that Claire was accompanying us, I think that he found lodgings for us to keep Claire out of his bed. She pouts continuously because he did not seem at all interested in seeing or speaking with her when he arrived at the hotel. He did not inquire about her health. Currently, she sulks in her room and plots new schemes to try to win his heart, assuming he has one to win. She is particularly offended because Byron invited Shelley and me to dine with him but the invitation excluded her. I fear that at some point she will confront him and make a scene. It's a good thing that they are both actors; in any case, no matter the outcome, I am certain that their theatrics will provide us with entertainment, after all, they've already rehearsed their roles at Hamlet and Ophelia.

12 June 1816

Shelley and Byron spend considerable time together on the lake. You would think that they are lovers. Perhaps they are. After all, Byron has been known for sexual dalliances with men. There are rumors about him and Polidari.

I sometimes feel a little jealous of the time that Shelley is away from me and the time that he is allotted for his creativity, but I have Willmouse and I have my own thoughts and writing and I deeply enjoy the magnificence and serenity of the lake when the weather is calm, as it has been for a few days; its many sailboats populate its azure waters. I find myself drifting along with the boats in absolute, pure peace. At such time, I sense that Shelley will not be the only one who will benefit from our sojourn here.

VINDICATED

The weather has turned calamitous again. It is so dark during mid-day that we must light candles. Byron and Shelley contribute to each other's black moods and Claire remains sulky and despondent. Last night, she and George got into a tremendous row about her pregnancy with her calling him a blackguard and him denouncing her as a strumpet. They battled for what seemed like hours, until they finally exhausted themselves and retreated to their fighting corners.

And, unfortunately, I have felt unwelcome because Byron has some very conventional and provincial opinions about woman's place in the world. I have argued with him, which is really against my nature, but I feel that I must stand up for my sex and let him know that we are full human beings and are capable of greatness, just as he is. He contends that "We get no Christ or Confucius from you; therefore, we get no poets, philosophers, or leaders from you." I am certain that others share his view but Shelley and I do not. As democratic as Byron claims to be, he is completely ignorant about sexual equality and the ways in which the long history of women's oppression, forced servility, and lack of equal education have kept us from realizing and enjoying our full humanity.

Perhaps he will change his mind, but being around Claire does not help the situation, because she plays the femme fatale or occasionally the sexual innocent, the weak and helpless girl. It's all a ploy to get him to go to bed with her once again.

I can't help but wonder why Byron is so anti-female. He seems a wounded creature. Perhaps he never received a mother's love. Perhaps because of his deformity his mother rejected him. I shall try to be more charitable to this wounded man, but he continually angers me because of his misogyny. I do not keep private company with him because of his loathing of women.

Polidori reports that he read in the *Times* that the weather is miserable because of a volcanic eruption last year and that the entire summer will be cold, wet, and blustery. All of my hopes for spending the summer on the lake have vanished. The time between tempests is brief and Byron and Shelley never seek any company when they are able to sail.

Their time together has been fruitful. Because of it, Shelley writes like a madman, penning "Mont Blanc" and his "Hymn to Intellectual Beauty." I am grateful that Byron's skepticism has not rubbed off on Shelley.

Due to the perpetually wet and tempestuous weather, Byron has come up with an indoor activity that he thinks will keep us amused. He suggests that each of us write a ghost story. To prepare and much to Claire's liking, we have been reading ghost stories, which seems entirely fitting, considering the somewhat Gothic nature of this house and the stormy environment. Lightning struck near the villa and an enormous alpine tree caught on fire. The winds howl continuously and darkness prevails. Thunder booms and rattles the windows.

Tonight, Byron read us Coleridge's "Christabel," which I have always found captivating, but Shelley became quite distraught when he began to envision a woman with nipples that were eyes. He suddenly cried out and raced from the room. I had to seek him out in the garden and calm his hysterics. He was acting like Claire usually does when she hears a frightful tale. I often fear that Shelley has lost his faculties, and tonight was one of those moments. But then he grows calm and appears perfectly sane. Madness and brilliance do sometimes seem interchangeable. It *is* the English malady and Shelley seems infected by it.

In addition to our reading of ghostly tales and poems, we also spend considerable time talking about human perfectibility and evolution. Shelley deeply believes that the new science, not just natural philosophy, and a type of philosophical alchemy, can effect human perfectibility. I am reminded of my mother's views that as humans grow in their knowledge of the intricacies of the universe and as we apply scientific principles to our lives, all human life will improve. Shelley and my mother hold the same beliefs in this regard. Byron is a skeptic, as am I, although I would like to see humanity become perfected by becoming more humane, compassionate, and just.

Shelley talked at length to the group about the galvanic experiments that we observed and I testified to the experiments that I witnessed. Afterwards, Byron suggested that we try to replicate the frog experiment. He hobbled out to the garden to catch a frog but only returned soaked. He seemed rather reptilian after his jaunt into the drenched garden and had to sit at length by the fire to dry out. I tried not to laugh at his folly.

16 June 1816

After our lengthy and disquieting discussions about human perfectibility, we went to bed in the wee hours and I tossed and turned. Sleep evaded me. I spoke with my mother who reminded me of her writing in her travel book about the humans that she met who seemed to have been only "half alive, made by Prometheus, when the fire he stole was so exhausted, that he could only spare a spark to give life." I ruminated on this and finally fell into a restless asleep. I suddenly awoke from a lurid night terror. I saw a creature stitched together by a human God, a Prometheus who had stolen, not fire, but bodies from their graves, like our Resurrectionists, and carved the bodies into pieces and then made a composite creature. The unhallowed creator, who eerily resembled my Shelley, knelt next to his creation, nearly worshipping the creature. He touched the creature's chest and then applied electrical current to the creature's lifeless and flaccid heart. The creature looked fair and beautiful before the electrical probe was applied to him. Miraculously, when the current was applied, like the frog, he jerked alive. He was awake and aware. But then a terrible transformation occurred. Once enlivened, his visage and unholy body became terrorizing and hideous, so hideous that the human creator fled from the room, fearful for his own life. He left the creature, whom he had deemed a monstrosity, utterly abandoned.

My dream disturbed me so much that I lay awake until dawn, worrying that the creature would emerge from the shadows. But I now knew what to write as my tale. As soon as the sun peeked over the mountain, I began to record my nightmare.

21 June 1816

Even though I was horrified, I sketched what I saw in my dream and then let it rest for a few hours as I thought about the philosophical aspects of the story. My Geneva-born hero will have a Faustian desire to transgress human limitations and engender life and a new species; to that end, he abandons all other pursuits. He no longer reads or writes poetry; he does not paint, sing, or dance. He does not visit nature's cathedrals, the forests and meadows. He is utterly obsessed with his aim to overcome death, all because his beloved mother has died and no one was able to save or resurrect her. Perhaps because he was overly protected, like the Buddha, he never witnessed death, not even the death of a beloved hound, until his mother was fetched in the night.

This young doctor, the new Prometheus, whom I shall call Victor, is vastly interested in occult philosophy via Cornelius Agrippa and dabbles in alchemy, even searching for the philosopher's stone. He is a bit like my Shelley in this regard. His professors believe that he is horribly misguided because he favors ancient and discredited occult practices over modern science. Nevertheless, he disregards their advice and pursues his dream to create a superhuman species that can overcome human limitations. His obsession is chronic, causing him to work tirelessly; for over two years, he rarely eats or sleeps. He abandons all friendships. He neglects his health. He neglects his soul. He does not realize that he cannot be a true philosophical alchemist because he has not purified himself as is necessary to transform base metal to gold or to perform any sort of true metamorphosis.

Victor believes that his action is warranted and aims toward the good of humanity; he believes that his creation will result in human perfection yet he cannot discern the consequences or implications of his act.

As I shape the trajectory of my story, I ponder certain essential questions. To what extent has Victor Frankenstein transgressed and angered the gods? What is his obligation to his creation? Is he, in his actions toward his creation, like a Deistic God who has created us and then abandoned us to survive on our own? Will the creature suffer because he has no mother, only a distant, disavowing father?

24 June 1816

The dismal weather continues unabated, which engendered the perfect setting for the reading of our stories. First, Byron narrated his story about a dying aristocrat. I wondered if perhaps he was referring to himself. What could he be hiding? Had his licentiousness finally caught up with him for good? I didn't have long to ponder my speculation, because as soon as Byron finished his tale and poured himself a tumbler of wine, Shelley started to read his short tale about "ghost chasing" and stealing bodies in Highgate Cemetery. I was the only one who knew that his story was autobiographical and I wondered if anyone would try to connect Shelley's tale to mine, which I was eager to read. I started to speak when Shelley laid down his manuscript but then Byron turned to Polidori and said, "John, please scare us silly. Shelley's story did not make me quiver. I found it rather comedic with all of the gravediggers stealing corpses and then heading straight to the pub."

Polidori looked smug, believing that for once he might best Shelley, whom he considers his rival for Byron's affection. He rose from the couch on which he was lounging and read his tale of Lord Ruthven who got drunk on blood. I began to wonder if all three of these stories were autobiographical and looked closely at Polidori to see if he cast a shadow. The candles barely illuminated the room so it was difficult to see. I felt a bit uneasy, but I tried not to think about it further. Surely vampyres were fiction but he wrote so convincingly that I feared that he had at least some experience with the Undead. When Polidori said "Fini," Byron, who acted as judge, said, "Marvelous. Now that sent chills through me. You scared me so that I may need to take Claire into my bed for comfort."

He looked at Claire, who was grinning as if she had won the contest. Shelley turned to Byron and said, "Stop jesting, George. Which story did you deem the best?"

"Why Mr. Polidori's, of course! I believe we have a winner."

Polidori smirked at Shelley and then reached out to Byron to grasp his hand.

"No, wait," I piped up, "I have a tale too."

Shelley seemed surprised and Byron looked at me oddly and smiled sardonically as if to say, *Little girl, how could you write a grisly tale equal to or better than what we have just heard?* I ignored his dismissive look and moved closer to the candlelight. The light flickered on the page, but then grew stronger, illuminating it.

My voice trembled as I began. "It was on a dreary night . . ." I had to stop. I had never read the tale aloud nor to anyone and reading it in near darkness with shadows surrounding us made me tremble even more. I tried to quiet my racing heart. I then looked at Shelley. His encouraging smile gave me confidence and I felt bathed in light. I began again. "It was on a dreary night in November, that I beheld the accomplishment of my toils. With an anxiety that almost amounted to agony, I collected the instruments of life around me, that I might infuse a spark of being into the lifeless thing that lay at my feet. It was already one in the morning; the rain pattered dismally against the panes, and my candle was nearly burnt out, when, by the glimmer of the half-extinguished light, I saw the dull yellow eye of the creature open . . . "

I heard gasps and I paused. Claire was grasping Shelley's arm and I saw that Byron had closed his eyes and folded his hands like a steeple in front of his chest. Shelley wore an anxious look; he nodded to me, indicating that I should proceed.

"How can I describe my emotions at this catastrophe, or how delineate the wretch whom with such infinite pains and care I had endeavoured to form? His limbs were in proportion, and I had selected his features as beautiful. Beautiful!—Great God! His yellow skin scarcely covered the work of muscles and arteries beneath; his hair was of a lustrous black, and flowing; his teeth of a pearly whiteness; but these luxuriances only formed a more horrid contrast with his watery eyes . . ."

I glanced up to see Polidori, Byron, Shelley, and Claire staring at me. Their eyes grew wide as they imagined the scene in the dismal room and young Victor's act of creation, a moment that belied and mocked the image of the act of creation as rendered by Michelangelo, when the creator imparts life by touching Adam's extended finger. Unlike Adam's creator, my creator touched his creature with profane hands, and thus his creature was a loathsome, vile replica of a man. His creature "became a thing such as even Dante could not have conceived."

I continued and revealed Victor's tortured dream, after he fled his creation, whereby he thought that his beloved cousin Elizabeth, whom he held in his arms, had been transformed into his dead mother, her shroud crawling with grave-worms. Claire shrieked and suddenly cried out, "No! It can't be!" I ignored her and proceeded as the candle momentarily sputtered as a gust of wind blew in from the veranda.

As I completed my tale, I felt an eerie presence. Like Victor, who fretted that the miserable monster remained in his apartment, I looked around to see if my creature had arrived in our midst. I saw shadows play against the wall but fortunately no creature emerged.

When I finished, I was shaking as indeed all in the room seemed to be. Claire looked horrified as did the rest of the audience who remained completely silent. Byron opened his eyes and for a brief second they looked like the dull eyes of Victor's creature.

"Mary, where did that tale come from?" Byron asked. "Did Shelley write that for you?"

"Of course not. It's solely a product of my imagination. My own dreams. I dreamt it," I replied. "As we know, we are such stuff as dreams are made on."

Byron laughed and then Shelley added, "And our little lives are rounded with a sleep."

Then Byron began to clap slowly and all joined in. "Well done!" he exclaimed. "I believe we have our winner."

I saw respect in his eyes for the first time. Although I wanted to, I refrained from saying, "You thought that a young girl could not write a grisly tale, didn't you? And you think that women are incapable of imagination. What's your opinion now of the female sex and our ability to exercise imagination? Are we not worthy writers?"

15 July 1816

I continue to write my story and now envision it as a novel, again, not one in the usual sense, with romantic figures and adventures, although there may be some to attract the reader, but one embedded in philosophical and theological ideas. I feel Milton's presence in this place, not that I imagine myself Milton rewriting *Paradise Lost*, but I do think about and consider Adam's queries of his creator, when he boldly asks,

> Did I request thee, Maker, from my clay
> To mould me man? Did I solicit thee
> From darkness to promote me?

My creature, who will be much maligned by his creator, also did not ask to be created. Like Adam, and all of us humans, he wonders why he was "moulded from the clay." What is the purpose of this creation and why has the creator abandoned him, left him on his own to learn, to attempt human connection, to try to become human?

12 August 1816

I've been a bit distracted from my work because we have heard
from my sister Fanny about my father's financial distress. He has
many debts. His publishing business is failing and Fanny asks
that we continue to support him so that he can do the work that
he was meant to do, to write his philosophical treatises and his
novels. She relates that he is currently working on another novel,
Mandeville, after traveling to Scotland to meet his friend Sir
Walter Scott. I won't complain about it to Shelley but I wonder
about his travel when he can ill afford to spend the money. I did
mention this to Claire but she reminded me that the three of us
did the same not long ago so that we cannot begrudge him what
he needs. For once, she seemed more reasonable than I.

Fanny also tells us that she has made plans to visit with our
mother's sisters Eliza and Everina in Ireland. I do hope that
she is well received and that her distress about father abates.
I have asked her to come to stay with us but she has declined
because she says that she does not feel that she could be part of
our group; even though she continues to express love for me,
she labels all of us libertines. She doesn't understand us and
has no desire to spend her days among us. She has heard about
our reputation as advocates of free love, even though we do not
necessarily exercise our philosophy. At least I don't. Perhaps she
is right. She doesn't fit in with Shelley, Claire, and me, but I still
love her. She is my mother's daughter and forever a part of me.

20 August 1816

We are returning to England. Shelley has secured a house for us
in Bath. As I expected, things did not work out as Claire had
hoped with Byron. Without a marriage proposal or at least an

engagement, we must hide her pregnancy and thus go where no one knows us. Much to her dislike, she will be sequestered until the child is born. She will be cloistered like the "nun" that her mother wished her to be.

We receive more ill news from Fanny who relates that our aunts refused her visit, all because of my sullied reputation. They think that I am a slattern and extend this condemnation to poor Fanny. I suppose that they condemn our mother too, even though Mother saved her sister Eliza, but this is completely unfair to Fanny. I may have unintentionally maligned my reputation, but my choices and actions should not reflect negatively on my sister. She is a pure soul, untouched by any male or female. Perhaps this contributes to her melancholy and loneliness. She has written that she loves me more than ever, because of my great worth, but also because the world has deserted me. The world meaning Father, I suppose. Once we arrive in Bath, I will reach out to her and bring her into our fold regardless of whether she wishes to be part of our circle. She is my sister and I must care for her. Like all creatures, she needs human affection and loving kindness.

30 August 1816

All of these family troubles bleed into my tale which unfolds rapidly. Although I have not completed my creation story, I can envision the other parts, particularly those scenes where Victor loses his mother and then other family members who are very dear to him. He will be punished for his transgressions but also for not caring for his creation, for not following Coleridge's edict to love the hideous and the unlovable. There is certainly a profound lesson in this narrative and now I am grateful that I heard and heeded Coleridge's frightful tale when I was a mere child, even though I sought my nursemaid, Miss Adela, for comfort at the time. Now, my tale and the act of creation provide some solace and make me feel whole.

8 September 1816

We are now in Bath and we have received more distressing news from Fanny. She appears personally distraught and keeps imploring us to do more for our father. We have sent him a substantial amount of money, several hundred pounds, and I've told her that this is all that we can do. She asks nothing for herself but I will soon journey to Bristol and fetch her to come live with us. Willmouse should know his auntie and the more that I write my novel, the more empathy I feel for those who feel unloved or neglected by those who are kin and who are under an obligation to care for one another.

25 September 1816

Willmouse has been sick with the sniffles and a cough so that I have not been able to retrieve my sister. I told her that I was coming but then had to postpone. She sends me alarming letters. She tells me that she has led a worthless, useless life. She seems quite despondent. I will send Shelley in my stead.

1 October 1816

Shelley has also been unable to travel because he has also been ill after catching Willmouse's malady. I instructed Fanny to please get on the train herself; I sent her the fare, but she has not responded. I am quite alarmed and as soon as Shelley has fully recovered, he promises that he will seek my sister and secure her well-being.

VINDICATED

8 October 1816

Shelley traveled on to Swansea today because the last letter that we received from Fanny indicated that she had moved farther from us into to Wales. The content of the letter suggested acute despair. When Shelley read it, he crumpled it up and said, "I must go now!" She claimed that she belongs nowhere and that her life has only caused pain to all who have known her. She is of no use to anyone and is redundant. She should never have been born. She is cursed. I told Shelley to make haste!

9 October 1816

Shelley reports that he found my sister unconscious in her hotel room. She had imbibed a full bottle of laudanum. Shelley shook her and called for help. She was not merely unconscious. She was dead. The proprietors fetched a physician who tried to revive her by emptying the contents of her stomach, but it was too late.

She left a note that said that her birth was unfortunate and that she hopes that she will soon be forgotten. My darling Fanny! You were our mother's love child and you thought that no one loved you.

When my mother heard of Fanny's demise, she wept bitterly and I endeavored to console her. I was unsuccessful.

How awful it must be to feel unloved. She did not know my deep affection for her; this is my fault; I should have told her and insisted that she join us. We would gladly have made her part of our circle, even if she thought us eccentrics and libertines.

I can't sleep due to a guilty heart. I wish that I had paid more attention to my sister's needs and that Shelley could have arrived in time to rescue her. Perhaps she thought that she was fulfilling what our mother failed to do when she was in great distress because of feeling unloved and abandoned by the world.

Perhaps, like our mother, she had a great need to love, but had no outlet for her affection.

15 October 1816

Because of Fanny's suicide, my father insisted that we not recover Fanny's body and therefore she was buried as a suicide in a pauper's grave!

Godwin and his wife have also insisted that no one learn about Fanny's self-destruction. Their rationale is that Fanny wished to live and die in obscurity and that we should abide by her wishes. They will publish a false account in the *Times* claiming that Fanny died of typhoid fever in Ireland. They are willing to lie in order to ensure their own unsullied reputations. I suppose that my father has forgotten that he and my mother were once considered scandalous.

My father has utterly failed as a revolutionary. He never used to care about what others thought of him. He wants to hide the truth that Fanny was an unhappy person who felt neglected by her family and the world. He wants to deny any role in her misery. She felt herself redundant and a burden. If only our mother had been here to advise her and to help her gain the education and confidence that could have ensured self-sufficiency. I wonder if Fanny ever tried to conjure our mother as I have. Perhaps if she had, she would have lived.

I vow that I will not be dependent on anyone, especially on a man. I will not be redundant or a burden. I am a writer; like my mother, I can survive by my pen if necessary.

14 November 1816

I have found it difficult to work on my novel, but Shelley writes prolifically and plans further projects. He continues to plan an epic drama, *Prometheus Unbound*, which will rail against Christianity, monogamy, and hypocrisy. It will be his most controversial work yet and is certain to create scandal and condemnation. Sometimes, scandal and condemnation seem his ultimate aims. We continue to discuss the Promethean myth and the ways in which knowledge is forbidden. Sometimes, like William Blake, I wish I had not acquired knowledge of evil. Life would surely be easier, if we were less aware of evil, but that is not possible. With consciousness, comes an awareness of evil and death. It is the human condition.

Surely, Fanny's suicide was an evil act, even though I don't think that a devil inspired it. The other evils in the world: war, famine, poverty, injustice, violence against women, and human ignorance must be overcome. I shall do my part to overcome ignorance through my writing and will wish for and try to effect a more perfect world where evil dare not show its face.

1 December 1816

I find that work helps me cope with my grief and guilt. I have completed Chapter Four, my creation story in my novel, and Shelley is delighted with it. For once, he has read my work! It turns on the notion that the creature, who has become hideous and will potentially resort to evil, may be an aspect of young Victor Frankenstein's soul. There is no denying that all of us, no matter how good, contain or have the propensity for evil. In denying evil within and in trying to create perfection, Victor has failed. Fortunately for him and unlike his creature, whom he has abandoned, Victor's friend, Henry Clerval the poet, finds Victor in his agitated mental state and nurses him to health. He feeds him, reads to him, and soothes his spirit. Clerval attempts to mother

Victor, but the poor, pitiful creature lacks a real mother. Perhaps this is his greatest loss and the reason that he will not thrive.

My story will dwell on the necessity of human connection and one's obligation to one's fellow creatures, even if they seem unworthy or less than human or unlovable.

I am not certain how we can withstand the news that Shelley received today. We were already emotionally wounded because of Fanny's self-destruction, but now we have learned of another consequential death. Shelley received a letter this morning from his friend Thomas Hookham. Harriet Shelley was found drowned on 10 December in the Serpentine Pond. A man walking his retriever through Hyde Park found her body, which had been in the pond for days. She was disfigured and mottled from the water. Her body was partially eaten. Apparently, she, like my sister, took her own life! I know at one time I thought that she should step aside but taking her own life was not the answer. It is awful to realize that she once threatened to commit suicide but Shelley and I believed that just a bit of theatrics. And I never got to know her as I had one day hoped. Perhaps we could have been friends, because of our mutual love of Shelley.

It also appears that she was eight months pregnant. So, not only did she forfeit her own life but she took the life of her child. How very sad and tragic. Thank God she did not become Medea and kill her other children as she once claimed she might do.

In a moment of selfishness, I questioned Shelley and asked if the unborn child was his but he retorted, "No. Do you think me a cad? I would never betray you." He claims not to have seen Harriet of late, except when he visited the children. But he had not seen the children since early November and it seems that Harriet had left them with her parents and had gone into hiding, using an assumed name of Harriet Smith. We believe that her parents, the Westbrooks, may have thrown her out of their home, telling her that she was an unfit mother, all because she was pregnant by a man other than Shelley.

Shelley is quite shaken. Still, he claims that he is not responsible for her death or unhappiness. I, on the other hand, do feel responsible. I know that I am Shelley's natural mate, but our union made Harriet extremely unhappy and this may have led to her self-destruction. I know how I would feel if Shelley abandoned me. I would be shattered, as was Harriet. I only see that now in the aftermath of her death.

I sometimes wish that I was a believer and if a believer, then a Roman Catholic. At least they have the ability to confess and seek forgiveness for the way they have injured others. I now wish that I would have told Harriet that I am sorry that we caused her such pain. Shelley tells me to forget about Harriet; Harriet chose to end her life; we did not force her to relinquish it. His only aim now is to secure custody of his children, Ianthe and Charles. He is adamant that they belong to us, not to the Westbrooks, who abhor Shelley and will likely forbid Shelley from seeing his own children.

I am beginning to wonder about the black cloud that seems to hang over our union. First Sophia, then Fanny, and now Harriet. To what extent are we liable for these premature deaths? Are the gods punishing us? Why does our love result in pain and death?

23 December 1816

Shelley's lawyers advise us that we should marry as quickly as possible, if we wish to obtain custody. Although we both believe that marriage is a flawed institution that results in legal bondage for women, we have agreed to proceed with the vows and I have notified my father. We shall see what his reaction is.

I still grieve for all of the recent loss, but now look forward to the possibility that our family will grow. That William will have a new brother and sister and that our love will overcome all of the heartache of recent days. Surely, the magistrate at the Chancery will rule in our favor, since Percy is the children's father; at least we know with certainty that he sired Ianthe.

30 December 1816

Today, I wore white at St. Mildred's Church, named after Mildred the Virgin. A statue of Mildred witnessed our vows. The irony was not lost to me.

The ceremony was modest. Both Shelley and I insisted on it. We exchanged brief vows according to the dictates of the Church of England. However, I did not consent to obey Shelley and to our amazement, the vicar agreed to exempt us from that part of the traditional vows.

My father and Mrs. Clairmont attended, which made the ceremony more official and sanctioned, although my father's reputation as a rebel will probably not help our cause to become the legal guardians of Shelley's children. I was happy to hear my father state that he believes that I have made a "good match" and that he has great hopes that Shelley will make me a suitable companion and husband. I was surprised at his reaction after his continued rejection of us and of our union. Perhaps he is coming around to caring for the two of us again. Yet we feel that he is a bit duplicitous. However, the witnesses to our ceremony can testify that we have family support for our marriage and that may help secure our custody case to the Lord Chancellor. I worry that

Godwin blesses our union only to ensure that we will continue to financially provide for him.

Although marriage seems unnecessary to me and I had hoped to live in a world where there was "neither marriage nor the giving in marriage," I feel relieved that Shelley and I are now joined properly. This will help us acquire the children and perhaps Claire will desist in her pursuit of my husband. I noted that she wept at the ceremony, certainly not for joy. Perhaps she will eventually realize that our union is strong, sanctioned by the church and government and can withstand any and all trials and tribulations and any attempt on her part to come between Shelley and me.

1817

11 January 1817

Claire complains of labor pains. We have called for her midwife, even though, based on my own experience, I doubt that Claire is far along in the birth process, although she does complain so and carries on like she is dying. Knowing what I know about the dangers of childbirth and the tragedies that can accompany it, I wish that I had more sympathy for her, but she did bring this on herself. She seemed to want Byron's child, in order to try to secure him, which did not work. For the life of me, I can't imagine wanting to be tied to him and his arrogance. In Claire's mind, he is a substitute for Shelley and yet he is so dissimilar to my love.

A new midwife attends Claire, because Mrs. Blenkinsop refused to attend Claire. She wouldn't say why but I suspect that Claire was rude and uncivil to Mrs. Blenkinsop and she won't tolerate fools. The new nurse, Miss Forsythe, tries to alleviate Claire's pain with laudanum, wine, and attaching a rope to the bed for her to pull on. Miss Forsythe also placed a knife under the bed to cut the pain and yet nothing appears to quell it. Claire screams every time her womb seizes.

Although it's difficult, I try to drown out her wailing by retreating to the garden to write. I continue to write my novel, which I now call *Frankenstein*. I have created a frame story with an adventure scene, which should entice readers. A young explorer, Captain Walton, who is endeavoring to discover a passage through the North Pole, fishes up our Victor from the icy sea. Victor has been chasing his creature and the creature has also pursued him. His creature taunts him and they are set to destroy one another. Victor, like the Ancient Mariner, needs to tell his tale to someone as recompense and Captain Walton seems like a suitable potential listener. He is someone who needs to hear that transgression, pursuing forbidden knowledge, may not be the best path towards human perfectibility or great achievement. Will Walton listen attentively and heed Victor's warning about what may happen if you exceed human limitations? Does Walton possess Victor's hubris? Is Victor penitent? Does he hope to make recompense to his creation?

I hear a great deal of pandemonium and shouting. I must stop writing. Claire is screaming my name and then "Bloody Byron" after that. I had best see if I can help her through the ordeal.

12 January 1817

After much tribulation, Claire has given birth to a baby girl, whom she has named Alba. The child is as pale as her name. Claire did have a difficult time birthing Alba. Shelley had to leave the flat because he could not stand to hear her wail endlessly for hours while cursing that "devil Byron." At least she is starting to realize his unworthiness so I felt more empathy for her, especially when the baby turned out to be breech and the midwife had Claire hang upside down as the midwife turned the baby head-down for the birth, a maneuver that caused Claire to bellow even louder.

Claire grasped my hand through most of the last part of the birth; I thought that she would break my fingers. The midwife and I told her to try to let her body do its work, to open up and not fight the labor. This did not help and all she could do was ask me over and over if she was going to die. I told her "No" but, of course, I didn't really know. All I could see was fear in her eyes. She looked like a frightened doe. I did my best to soothe her but nothing helped much. She thrashed about and continued to wail like her own banshee foreseeing her own death.

When Alba emerged, she was still in her caul. The midwife gasped and said, "The child wears the veil." Apparently, "wearing the veil" is quite rare and, according to the midwife, is considered good luck. Perhaps Alba will be an extraordinary child and woman. My immediate thought was not as positive; perhaps her heritage is a blight and it will smother her. I, for one, can't help but think that the "veil" is a bad omen.

Once the midwife lifted the veil and cleaned up Baby Alba, she placed her in Claire's arms. With her baby in her arms, she seems content and is an attentive mother. She stopped cursing Byron and instructed Shelley to write to Byron and to tell him that his child was safely delivered, not that he would care.

I do understand though that a mother's love is great and perhaps loving little Alba will be what Claire needs to grow toward a greater humanity, to become more perfectly human.

It is our Willmouse's birthday. How he has grown in the last year! He takes a few steps of late, back and forth between Shelley and me. And he says Mama when he falls and lands in my arms. I am grateful to the universe for giving me this little mouse and for his continued good health. We blew out the birthday candle on the tiny cake that our new servant Elise baked for him, wishing away all sickness and bad fortune. It was festive and Shelley and I have grown closer through our love of our Willmouse.

We have been staying in London with our friend Leigh Hunt because Shelley was required to testify in court and we wish to be close by to hear the Chancery's decision in regard to custody of Ianthe and Charles. It is exceedingly difficult to await the decision, but I remind Shelley that patience remains a virtue. We try to stay hopeful that all will turn out well and that the children will soon join us in in our new home in Marlowe. Shelley has asked the proprietor to prepare cheerful rooms for them and a nursery for all of the children. The hobby horse awaits them as do picture books, a telescope where they can gaze at and dream about infinite worlds, and a delightful kaleidoscope that further engenders the imagination. Ianthe has a special bed prepared for her that has a large canopy. I caution Shelley not to go overboard or to insist that Ianthe possess feminine objects that will enfeeble her, but he says that his children will not want for any material or emotional needs. However, he promises to remain mindful to not weaken Ianthe by excessive attention to trivial things.

He, of course, possessed all of the material needs that he required as a child, but his emotional needs were not met; his father was distant and cold. Shelley is an observant, loving father to Willmouse and promises to be the same for Charles and Ianthe. They will greatly benefit from the love and education that we can give them. We will raise them to be creative, free spirits; they will run and play and study under our guidance. We will raise Ianthe as our own daughter and follow my mother's precepts in regard to the education of her.

We are delighted that the young poet John Keats has also arrived to stay with the Hunts for a few days. Although some critics disparage Keats's poetry, calling him a cockney upstart, a mongrel who uses simplistic vernacular, Shelley thinks highly of Keats's work and considers him his protégé. He and Shelley spoke at length about Spenser's "Faerie Queen," the poem that Keats claims awakened his imagination and led to his own poetry. Keats's first volume of poetry is being published by Shelley's publisher and Shelley has enthusiastically read the poems but has advised Keats to take his time to publish further until his work has matured. Keats seems, according to Shelley, to be in a hurry to publish, although we can't understand why. I favor Shelley's friendship with Keats over his companionship with Lord Byron. Like Shelley, I am very taken with Keats's "On First Looking into Chapman's Homer," which moves us to understand that translation is interpretation; if done well, we see the ancient world for the first time, even if we have entered those golden worlds many times in the poems and histories that we read. I must keep this in mind whenever I take on the task of translation; it is an art, not a transcription.

While Shelley and Keats roam the Heath, I spend time in the garden on a bench under the weeping willows and continue to work on my creation. Of late, my creature appears before me in all of his hideousness, but I have much empathy for him and have grown in my affection for him. I often identify with him and with his motherless state, his rejection by his creator, his need for human relationships. He cannot help his physical being and he never asked to be "born." He is a bit like all of us humans actually. As he stands before me, he also asks me why I created him. I tell him that he was born of a dream, a nightmare actually, and dreams, like life, are not under our control. From where they emanate no one knows. He seems puzzled by this because he does not know what dreams are. He seemed shocked when I told him that while we sleep images and scenes arise before our eyes and we can often see our loved ones. He remarked that his sleep is dreamless and then asked, "Please, Can you give me the gift of dreams?" Sadly, I replied, "No that is beyond my abilities. I can conjure characters and worlds but cannot determine all of their capabilities." He looked disappointed, bowed to me, and walked away into the woods behind our house.

As I write, I see Victor's creation as a flawed but potentially benevolent being. He is half-formed, but aren't we all? He is resourceful and after his abandonment by his creator, he has attached himself to a formerly noble family, the De Laceys, in France, although they do not know that he is their benefactor and sometimes their voyeur or that he is learning language and literature from them. He is a quick learner and has even read the entirety of *Paradise Lost* and *Paradise Regained*. He told me that he admires Milton's poem "Lycidas," because it laments the loss of a beloved friend. He has also read Plutarch's *Lives*, much like myself. Although that may seem absurd, it seems reasonable to me. How else might he learn about the human potential for nobility and greatness? About beneficence and everlasting friendship?

The humans who encounter him do not understand that he, like them, must also be loved.

VINDICATED

My novel is more than an examination of human transgression; it's an exploration of what has been termed human nature. Are we inherently evil as Hobbes says or are we inherently good, like Rousseau's natural man? If one were to create a human-like creature would that creature inherit an innately good or evil nature? In his observation of humans, will he be taught evil or good ways? How much of our reaction to any creature depends upon that creature's physical beauty or lack thereof? Why do we associate evil with the hideous and the deformed? Why do we fear those who are alien or atrocious to us?

17 March 1817

Today ought to be a day of joy, but once again it is a time of profound mourning. The Lord Chancellor has ruled against Shelley in the custody battle. He has labeled him unfit, "immoral in principle and conduct." Shelley's past haunts him, particularly his refusal to deny that he and Thomas Hogg wrote and distributed "The Necessity of Atheism." Shelley's own poetry is also held against him; the Lord Chancellor deemed "Queen Mab" atheistical and immoral in its condemnation of religion and royalty and its argument about human perfectibility here on earth, its advocacy that there is no need for a heaven. Our own relationship, even though we are now legally bound to each other, was also pronounced immoral because we had lived as wife and husband prior to our marriage. The Lord Chancellor also labelled Shelley an adulterer and a near bigamist. If these are the grounds to keep fathers from their children, then half of English landowners should be deemed unfit fathers. How many "bastard" children roam our village lanes?

In the end, he proclaimed that Shelley would raise the children to be atheists, which would in the end destine the children to live immorally and lead to their perdition.

I try to console Shelley but he tells me to leave him alone. He has shut himself in his study and sits in the dark with the curtains closed. He can't bear the thought that the court gave his children to a clergyman in Kent; that they will grow up having dogma forced down their throats on a daily basis, that they will "eat" Church of England tenets, that they will likely not have the freedom to exercise their imaginations, that they will not experience their own father's love. He fears that they will be taught to detest him and his work and that eventually they will forget him completely. He will be distant and cold, like his own father, but not through a lack of fatherly devotion, but through the court's ruling that forbids him from visiting his own children.

I feel great loss also; I had hoped for a house of laughter and love. Now we must shut the doors to their bedrooms, put away the new toys: the telescope and the kaleidoscope. Perhaps we will be able to send them as Christmas gifts once our fractured hearts have healed.

29 March 1817

As I suspected but did not tell Shelley, I am again going to bear a child. I will tell him soon, once his grief is partially assuaged. Perhaps this new child will help heal our hearts of the grief and the guilt that lays heavily upon them.

1 April 1817

Shelley and I have both thrown ourselves into our work. My narrative continues to unfold. My misunderstood creature has enacted revenge against his "father" and threatens more violence unless his creator agrees to provide him with a companion, another being similar to himself. Again, he has stood before me dripping with repulsiveness, wearing his rags, smiling his gruesome smile. Now, he beseeches me to ask the maker for a mate for him. His arguments are sound. Every creature has its mate, even loathsome snakes, frogs, toads, reptiles of all sorts. He has seen them cavorting in the woods. Why should he be deprived of affection and even intimate relations? I have no answer and cannot justify leaving him alone without a companion. I will offer his request to Frankenstein and await his reply.

2 April 1817

I was astonished that Victor agreed to fashion another half-formed creature given his animosity toward his creation. The creature's reasonable arguments must have persuaded him. Perhaps he thinks that by providing the creature with his own companion, the creature will leave him alone.

Victor has gathered his chemicals and instruments and has left for England to study how to fashion this new Eve. His dutiful and benevolent friend Clerval, accompanies him, although Frankenstein plans to travel far north to the Orkney Islands to find his filthy workshop and fashion a female creature. The wild, barbarous place where the wind bellows and blows continuously, the isolated environment, seems the perfect location to him to undertake his fulsome work. I watch him dig up the graves like a Resurrectionist in the middle of the night and snatch body parts to fabricate his new "Eve." The creature is never far away and watches Victor's every move. Victor is unaware of his voyeur. I think that he relishes his work, although he fears what the creation will become. Will his original creature be able to reproduce itself once it meets its mate and then populate the world? Although the creature promises to leave England and live in the jungles of South America, will he do that or will he and his new "Eve" remain here and terrify our world with their repulsiveness? Will the female even accept the creature as its mate or will it too reject him because he is so loathsome? Perhaps she will be more fearsome than he is. These are Frankenstein's and my worries.

This Eve is far different from the one that my mother imagines engendering in a new world. I read passages of my work to her and even though she finds all of my fictional world fearsome, she assents, and tells me that I have invented a new genre, a philosophical fiction, a science fiction. I have combined my love of philosophy with Shelley's search for the philosopher's stone, his quest to be an alchemist that transforms the world.

17 April 1817

Another spring is upon us and Willmouse and I spend happy hours in the garden watching the daffodils unfold in all of their glory. I try not to think of my sweet Sophia who lies cold in her grave next to my mother. I wish that I could pray for the good health of this child in my womb. I send her or him loving thoughts and talk to the child daily, reminding them to grow and blossom like the yellow buttercup daffies. I promise the child that I will take them to fields of daffodils next spring and we will feast on the magnificence that surrounds us.

20 April 1817

My narrative is drawing to a close. I was not surprised when the creature lashed out at Frankenstein when he furiously destroyed the half-formed new Eve. Victor's violence verged on rape. He seemed to be striking out at his abhorred creature. Frankenstein allowed his worries about the female's potential fearsomeness to overtake him and he envisioned that this new Adam and Eve could populate the earth with their deadly offspring.

In the wake of the destruction of his mate, the creature vowed ultimate revenge and set out to destroy everyone that Frankenstein loves. Lack of acceptance and love only engenders horrific violence. Even before his mate was destroyed, the creature strangled Victor's little brother, William, but then after witnessing the savaging of his mate by Frankenstein, he murdered the good, innocent Clerval. Finally, he vowed that he would be with Frankenstein on his wedding night and Frankenstein, being as obtuse as he is, did not understand that his beloved bride, his cousin Elizabeth, was in grave danger. Before Frankenstein could consummate his love with his bride, the creature strangled her, leaving her dead on her wedding bed. Now, Victor too is bereft and alone, just like his creature. Perhaps that will make him understand the creature's loneliness and grief.

The creature does understand right from wrong; he is not amoral. And he acknowledges that this "passion is detrimental" to him but his fury knows no bounds. Sadly, Victor's passion is also awakened. From the moment of the creature's "birth," Victor has always wanted to destroy his creature, but he now chases him through the northern wilds, with the creature egging him on, taunting him. I fear that no good will come from this and that both the creature and the creator will never be satisfied with the outcome. I sense that the creature still desperately longs for his creator's love but Frankenstein will surely never give it now that the creature has fulfilled Frankenstein's assumptions and prophecy about him. He abides in evil and Frankenstein cannot rise above his human condition. He has identified with Milton's Satan, but unfortunately, the creature has too. Unlike Satan, neither of them can make a "heaven of hell, a hell of heaven."

14 May 1817

My novel is complete. Tragically, the creature who was never loved or understood climbed upon his funeral pyre and took his own life, after he had hounded and destroyed his creator. As Frankenstein died, the creature wept.

I ponder the outcome and only conclude that the creator missed teaching and perhaps learning from his half-formed creation. Assuming god-like activities requires god-like beneficence. But once again, I always wonder about the Christian God's supposed benevolence. If he is omniscient and omnipotent, why does evil exist? Why does he allow it? Why are we born to die? What is the purpose in all of this human tragedy? I hope that my readers will understand and learn from the mistakes that Victor made. Although I dislike admitting it, some knowledge should be forbidden. Shelley does not agree, but he does admire my book, which he read quickly and endorsed. I have finally written something that Shelley has read in its entirety.

I now seek a publisher.

21 May 1817

Willmouse and I have been staying with Godwin and Mrs. Clairmont in London as I visit various publishers to show them my manuscript. Living with Father and Mrs. Clairmont has been more pleasant than I imagined. My father seemingly no longer harbors ill will toward Shelley and me and he delights in his grandson. My stepmother leaves me alone, which I prefer.

Godwin and I will likely never be as close as we once were, but there are occasional conversational moments that feel like the intellectual haven that we once shared, especially when Mrs. Clairmont is away making calls on her friends.

Willmouse's vocabulary has grown considerably and his grandfather spends hours reading to him and spinning tales for the child. I have never seen my father so whimsical and playful. Perhaps his publication of children's literature has had a positive effect on the cranky, old Prospero. His heart has surely grown several sizes as he has assumed the role of the wise man grandfather.

10 June 1817

I have been re-reading "Childe Harold." It makes me melancholy. It is perhaps not suitable for reading when one is nearing one's confinement. Even though Harold relishes the natural world, he is far too much of a misanthrope for my liking.

30 June 1817

I have obtained a publisher—Lackington, Hughes, Harding, Mavor and Jones. Because I am a woman and due to the nature of my novel, they have insisted that I publish my novel anonymously. I told them that Eliza Haywood, Frances Burney, and my mother did not publish anonymously or use pennames. I find the publisher's demand offensive and do not see why I cannot attach my name to the manuscript. The manuscript is mine. I do not want the authorship to be falsely attributed to another, especially a man. I argued with my publishers about the authorship issue but they did not relent. How will we women ever be taken seriously and be able to prove our creative genius, if we cannot attach our own names to our work?

Shelley tells me to me patient. He believes that the book will go into a second printing and that at that time I can reveal my authorship. In the meantime, I worry that its authorship will perhaps be falsely attributed to him just because he is a man and a published writer. I have dedicated the novel to my father so naturally it might be assumed that Shelley is the author because he is Godwin's most famous or infamous disciple.

15 July 1817

More rumors swirl around us. The gossips claim that Alba is Shelley's, not Byron's, daughter. Claire hungered for Shelley but they both insist that they have never had relations, although Shelley is overly fond of my stepsister. He particularly loves her melodic voice, which she has developed through her singing lessons and which he likens to an Aeolian harp. She does sing beautifully, but he insists that this is not enough for him to take her to his bed. Her voice is not reflective of her entire being; it is at odds with it. However, he calls her Constantina because of her constant and consistently extraordinary voice. I think of her as constant also, but her constancy is the result of her continuing to hang on to us, leech that she is. I know that I should be more charitable and love Claire, but I find it nearly impossible.

I grow tired of her and sometimes tired of myself and worry that these ill feelings will affect the child that grows in my womb. I must think of pleasant rather than hateful thoughts so that the seeds of animosity don't affect her well-being. Again, I feel certain that this child is a girl. I will have a second chance to raise a daughter as my mother would want, although my mother did worry about bearing girl children because, if properly and fully educated, they may be deemed unfit for the current world in which we live. I acknowledge this concern and often discuss it with my mother, but I will do my very best to educate my daughter while re-fashioning the world so that it accepts her knowledge and brilliance as natural.

10 August 1817

Shelley spends considerable time on his skiff floating on the lake and dreaming of other worlds. He writes like a fiend, composing a new poem, "The Revolt of Islam," which is inspired by Spenser but dwells on the doctrines of liberty and justice. It reflects on a wrongly-executed French Revolution, a revolution that betrayed its promise and ideals. I have provided Shelley with a thorough critique of his work as I always do.

I am confined now, awaiting the arrival of the child. I too wish that I could float about on the boat or on wispy clouds and look down on the green world like Milton's Eve. I feel in limbo as I await the grand entrance of this child. Why must women be confined when they are about to experience childbirth? Are we thought shameful? Society never wishes to acknowledge the fecund, gravid body. It finds this body repulsive, unnatural, and sinful. I find it exquisite.

1 September 1817

A baby girl is in my arms! She is a beautiful, wholesome child. She has all of her fingers and toes, and a wee nose. Her cheeks are ruddy and she has a robust cry. She seems quite sturdy. Thank God she doesn't seem to have been harmed so far by my tortured thoughts that occupied my mind towards the end of my pregnancy. I am not necessarily given to "old wives' tales," but the Irish in particular believe that what you think and observe can affect a pregnancy. They go so far as to think that, if you see a chicken at a certain point of the pregnancy, your baby will look like a chicken! These folk beliefs are amusing but also rather illustrative of the ways the old ways hang on in a scientific era. Perhaps I should collect these tales and publish them.

At any rate, although I am not completely taken with the idea, Shelley wishes to call her Clara after our Claire. Clara means bright and clear; she is akin to a bright new star; the sheen on her soft baby skin actually seems to glow, so I will not oppose naming her this. At least her name will not be Claire.

15 September 1817

Sweet Clara Everina never leaves my side, almost like her namesake! I found this effective with Willmouse; I have kept a watchful eye on him and he has had no illnesses aside from the short respiratory ones that all children acquire. Shelley thinks that I shield the children too much and that I'll smother them with too much love. I contest that, since one can never experience too much motherly love. I never experienced it as a child so sometimes I wonder where the deep affection for my children comes from. Perhaps my mother showers all of us with her love and I extend it to my children. I meet her frequently in my dreams and in the broad light of day and am grateful for her love.

I promise my children daily that no harm will come to them. I nurse my own child, knowing that a mother's milk is the best medicine that a mother can give her child.

3 October 1817

I can't understand why trouble continues to plague us. Harriet's creditors hound Shelley and they are threatening to imprison him! To prevent this, we have agreed once again that he should remain in hiding in London until all of this is sorted out.

In addition, although the children remain well, Shelley's health is in jeopardy. He experiences night sweats, which could indicate consumption, the malady that plagues so many these days, including our beloved friend Keats. We think that it would be best to travel to Italy for Shelley's health, but we can ill afford to do that currently. He must stay put and is unfortunately holed up in a dank, mildewed basement flat far from Marlowe near Russell Square in London. He reports that he occasionally sneaks out in disguise and studies in the British Library. I would love to see him sporting a false wig and mustache; perhaps he can be a secret agent like Christopher Marlowe! If so, let us hope that his end does not parallel Marlowe's own tragic demise.

20 October 1817

I have sent Shelley news that the creditors have visited our home in Marlowe, inquiring about his whereabouts. I kept mum and pretended that Shelley had abandoned me. The creditors had no trouble believing that, since they are aware of his relationship with Harriet. It is disquieting, when I consider how he deserted her for me. Would he do the same, if he grew weary of me? Or found me lacking as he did Harriet? Will I always remain his child of light? I have said that I will never grovel to keep him and that I can be independent and make my way in the world, but I don't necessarily wish to have to exercise that ability. I still love my Shelley, despite his faults, his occasional melancholy and mad choleric attacks. He is mine; I am his.

2 November 1817

We must quit Marlowe; the house is unhealthy. All of our books are molding; the air is fetid, which perhaps contributed to Shelley's cough. Once Shelley and I are reunited in London we must think of a way to relocate to Italy for the sake of everyone's health, not just Shelley's.

15 November 1817

Clara is now two and one-half months old. Today, she smiled at me for the first time. I know that some say that babies this age don't smile; they merely pass wind and that turns up the corners of their mouths. That is simply not true. She gazed right at my face this morning and smiled at her mama. Elise, the nursemaid, witnessed it so I wasn't the only one to be graced by Clara's affection.

Willmouse is an excellent big brother. Although a mere toddler, he takes responsibility for his wee sis and wants to hold her. I sit him on my lap and Elise hands Baby Clara to me and I help Willmouse cradle his sister. I sing her songs, such as "Where are you going, my pretty little maid?" which helps her fall asleep, and Willmouse tries to sing along.

I try not to think of Clara as the rebirth of Sophia. I possessed Sophia for such a short time. I still dream of her though and see her and Clara frolicking in a field of daffodils and bryony. They giggle and run about, chasing butterflies. My mother sits atop a hill and gazes at them, knowing that they are her blood and she beams at me, letting me know that she approves. Of course, it's just a dream, but some speculate that dreams are just another alternate reality, where we live out what might have been or will be. In any case, I am always happy to see my mother and Sophia in my dream-world. I feel blessed when they appear.

VINDICATED

4 December 1817

I have found a new flat in London and Shelley has been able to come out of hiding. His barrister has managed to satisfy the creditors and Shelley is no longer in danger of imprisonment. I worried very much that imprisonment would kill him both physically and spiritually. I am so pleased to have him back in our world and in my bed, where he belongs.

He is also happy because while in disguise he found a publisher for his "The Revolt of Islam." I am certain that when Shelley doffed his blonde wig the publishers had a hearty laugh to know who was hidden beneath the elegantly coiffed hair.

24 December 1817

Although we are certainly not Christians, we do celebrate the winter solstice and light the yule log. Some traditions are worth keeping and we think that it is healthy for the children to partake in the old ways that sustained our ancestors for centuries. At such times, we tell tales, just like the French do during the dark months of Toussaint. Tonight, Shelley told the children the story of the fairy queen, embellishing it with his version that harkens back to his Queen Mab who predicts a glorious future for humanity.

We are hoping that the impending year will be good for us and that our troubles will vanish completely, just as if fairy dust was blown on them. I know that this is whimsical but I must have hope.

27 December 1817

Sadly, the Christmas gifts that we sent to Charles and Ianthe have been returned to us with a note that asks us to please refrain from sending gifts or communicating any further with the children.

Shelley didn't say a word; he ripped up the note, threw it in the fire, and then stormed out of the flat.

1818

1 January 1818

My publishers have sent me copies of my *Frankenstein*, which appears in three volumes. The first has been released to the public. I feel proud of my creation and am elated that it found a home. The New Year begins well. Perhaps all of the pain of the last few years will dissipate and we will begin again.

17 January 1818

A new story percolates in my imagination. I spend considerable time thinking about and wishing to escape to Italy; both for Shelley's health and for our emotional well-being. I intend to set my story there but in earlier times, perhaps the medieval period. I have little time to write because of my duties to my children and my husband, but I jot down ideas and will let these schemes simmer as they arise. I have heard recently of the exciting notion of what is called lucid dreaming where you imagine a scene so vividly that in your real dreams you are transported there. I shall try this and see if I can be conveyed in my dreams to medieval Italy. Perhaps the Medicis will enter my dreams or one of the lecherous popes! I find Catholicism and all of its flaws fascinating, but more importantly, I am interested in how the growing desire for liberty in the medieval period is similar to our own time's longing.

VINDICATED

I continue to dream of Italy and have tried lucid dreaming. I see a medieval soldier of whom I have read; his name is Castruccio Castracani and he is the lord of Lucca. I see him with his lover Euthanasia. They cavort in her gardens at her fortress Valperga. They were once childhood playmates and sweethearts, but, like Romeo and Juliet, politics interferes with their love bond. But, in addition, the desire for personal power intercedes and affects their relationship.

My daydreams become more vivid as we make our plans to relocate and live in Italy. The very thought of the Tuscan sun piques my imagination and fuels my desire to dwell among the vineyards and hear the vinedressers sing their love songs. It also makes me happy because I know that Shelley and my children will thrive there away from the pestilence that is England, its eternal dampness and cold, its rigid social and political codes, as well as away from our unhappiness and ill fortune that have plagued us while we remain in England.

Once again, Claire is our constant companion. She will travel with us along with Alba. Claire wishes to see Byron and will endeavor one more time to make him grow enthralled with her or at least for him to care for or perhaps love his daughter. I don't see how this will happen. Claire's feminine wiles have failed in the past with George. She lacks sufficient charm and intellect. Perhaps she will try singing to him and he will fall deeply and everlastingly in love with her because of her angelic voice. It is doubtful, but this particular charm has worked on Shelley at least to the extent that her voice transports him to heavenly places.

1 March 1818

Last evening we toasted the publication of my *Frankenstein*. Although I rarely imbibe, I allowed myself one glass of champagne to celebrate the birth of my novel.

12 March 1818

We have set sail to Calais with Claire and the three children. The Ides of March are impending and once again the crossing is rough. I keep my children close so that they do not get buffeted about. Shelley must have a cast-iron stomach because he once again sits on the deck and gazes at the tortuous waves. I think that he is part merman. He loves the sea and always says that he feels part of it. Its sublimity enlarges his soul, just as the grand mountains do.

26 March 1818

We have arrived once more at the most beautiful lake in Europe, Lago di Como, Lake Como, a splendid place, at the foot of the Alps. We spent a brief sojourn here in 1816 and it inspired me to set Victor and Elizabeth's wedding there in *Frankenstein*. I expect that no tragedy will befall us as it did them in their fictional world. We hope to locate a home in this earthly paradise.

The weather is perfect; the sky is azure blue and delicate white clouds dot the sky. The sun is our daily companion and Shelley recuperates well; his cough has subsided and he spends most of his time on the lake. The children and I have joined him in some of his sailing. We rented a small craft. Shelley is such an expert sailor. He promises me that he will teach Willmouse and Clara to sail. Will is acquiring sea-legs and, like his father, dons a seafarer's cap.

Claire has traveled to Milan and I am glad to be alone with my family. Fortunately, she is occupied with communicating with Lord Byron who insists that Alba's name be changed to Allegra. God only knows why. I suppose that he thinks Allegra more romantic, just as Jane prefers to call herself Claire. Perhaps by bestowing a new name on the child, he will truly take an interest in her. I doubt his sincerity.

30 March 1818

While Shelley sailed alone today, the children and I visited Villa Melzi d'Eril with its stupendous Japanese garden filled with colossal and exquisite pink and purple rhododendrons. Afterwards, we took a carriage ride to a local farm and we ate olives, cheese, and salami. I am teaching Willmouse Italian and he says "Più formaggio per favore" with gusto. We are becoming *vero italiano*!

We continue to search for a home to rent, but so far, have found nothing suitable. Lake Como has perennially been the playground for the rich and famous ever since Roman times. We are neither and will probably have to move along to less exquisite surroundings. For now, Shelley and I and the children relish our time here and feel quite renewed. I continue to dream of medieval Italy and the romance and adventure associated with it. Shelley and I read Petrarch to each other and fantasize about being *amanti italiani*, Italian lovers!

10 April 1818

We have traveled to Milan to find an incessantly miserable Claire. She has finally discerned that Byron desires nothing from her other than taking Allegra from her. She rants about this absurd request. At first he wanted nothing to do with the child but, now, after a brief visit with her, he insists that Allegra is his and would be better off with him and would, in his care, become an aristocrat. Claire has responded to Byron's request with a resolute "No" and yet he persists. I believe that she still holds out hope that Byron will make her his Lady; she is delusional. He has never desired her and he cannot be faithful to one woman. He has many Italian lovers, which has made Claire livid.

I do not understand his motivation to take the child from Claire. Isn't it enough that he laid claim to her by changing her name? To which Claire acquiesces, even though she finds it difficult to adapt to. What can he gain by taking her other than a dependent? Besides, in her own way, she does love Allegra. Maternity ought to take precedence over paternity, but we do not live in equal times, despite the revolutions that spread all over Europe. The sexual revolution has not transpired along with the political one that sought liberty. Genuine liberty would entail true equal rights for women. But equal rights depend upon equal education and access to occupations and professions. Unfortunately, my mother's advocacy for equal sexual rights has not taken hold. I do credit my father with making my mother's writings available, even including her fiction, which are narratives that apply her ideas in *Vindication*.

10 May 1818

Shelley has interceded on behalf of Claire and has written to Byron, trying to persuade him to give up his demand that Allegra join his household. Shelley maintains that the child is better off with us because she is familiar with us and all of us love her. Byron does not know the child nor does he care for her. As Byron's friend, Shelley thinks that he can convince Byron to give up his quest.

VINDICATED

After much consternation and many tears, and despite our arguments to the contrary, Claire has agreed to Byron's demand. She thinks that Allegra will be better off in the long run because she will be raised as an aristocrat and will have all of the advantages that go with her title. Shelley is at odds with Byron over this. Shelley was raised to be the next baronet but found no real advantage other than the financial allowance that permitted him to travel. It surprises him that Byron maintains his title as a lord; he wants to believe that Byron is a republican but this indicates that in his heart, assuming he has one, he is not.

2 June 1818

I have been playing around with an opening scene in my new work, after having completed a considerable amount of historical research, including perusing archival material, about Castruccio. Castruccio, who will become lord of Lucca, will be exiled with his family as a child because of their strong aristocratic beliefs in a time that favors liberty for all. He will, on his own, visit an exhibition that parodies hell and then will witness a literal hell when a bridge collapses and hundreds of onlookers perish. Dante's *Inferno* will become reality for him and all who witness this horror.

11 June 1818

Shelley and I have secured lodgings in Bagni di Lucca, a resort village with a thermal spring, which ought to greatly benefit Shelley's health. It was the summer residence of Napoleon, which certainly doesn't positively influence our choice. It resembles Bath with its mineral springs but far exceeds Bath in terms of its beauty.

We hope to stay for the entire summer season and will settle in to write and read. Shelley will partake of its waters and will also be able to boat on the Serchio River and perhaps the children and I will be welcome on his skiff.

22 June 1818

I find this place tranquil as does Shelley. His health has improved as has his mood. He boats daily on the river and works on translating the *Symposium*. I continue to plan my new work, *Valperga*, imagining its fortress. The devil's bridge, Ponte del Diavolo, which was renovated by Castracani in 1300 A.D., near Bagni di Lucca, is a perfect model for my scene where the bridge collapses and plunges everyone into hell. I try to imagine a medieval worldview, one in which all hierarchies are in place from God to seraphim, to cherubim, to man, to woman. When I imagine it, I realize that this world is still very much intact in many places, despite the French and American Revolutions.

30 June 1818

The reviews of *Frankenstein* arrived today and my hands shook as I opened the envelope. I was eager for good news but, as we know, one bad review colors all of the positive ones. I saw this often enough with my father. So, I looked with trepidation at the various reviews from the *Edinburgh Review* to *The Gentleman's Magazine* to *The Quarterly Review*. Some reviewers herald it as a new form of the novel, as I had hoped; they call it "bold fiction," "original" and "excellent in language." I was so pleased to learn that Sir Walter Scott views the novel favorably. Of course, he is friends with my father but he doesn't know that I am the author, only that I dedicated it to Godwin. He wrote that the "work impresses us with a high idea of the author's original genius and happy power of expression." Another reviewer says that the novel is "the production of no ordinary writer." However, some condemn it, calling the novel a "horrible and disgusting absurdity" and asks if the author is as "mad as his hero." This reviewer also says that "it is written in the spirit of Mr. Godwin's school," and thus worthy of condemnation because it is similar to his writing. Perhaps they attribute the novel to Shelley as I feared. However, Shelley himself wrote a review, even though I asked him not to, since he surely has no objective lens with which to evaluate the book. I suppose though that it is helpful that he has written a review, which will prove that he is not the author. He need not boast about his own work; others can do that for him.

I find the mixed reviews a bit disheartening. It is always hard to hear criticism of something that you have labored over at length and about which you deeply care. The fictional world becomes a reality to the author. It is most troubling to me that one reviewer worries that readers will not necessarily walk away with a condemnatory message about human transgression. I do not believe that I could have been clearer in my intention. Frankenstein warns Walton repeatedly about exceeding human limitations. Victor has failed to produce anything resembling a real human being, although he has also failed by not caring for his creation. I give readers far more credit than does this reviewer.

Regardless, whether they extol or condemn the novel, all of the reviewers find it powerful enough to produce a lasting effect on the reader. I am pleased overall with this outcome and am encouraged to continue to exercise my imagination in ways that will bring about a more just world. I sense that *Frankenstein* will have a long life and that my writing will have an impact. My mother assures me that she knows that my work will succeed and that many generations will be both terrified and moved by it.

20 July 1818

Claire's drama is relentless. This time I do feel her plight. Now that Byron has seized Allegra he has placed her in Venice with a stranger, the wife of the British consul. He doesn't even visit the child and he refuses to allow Claire to see Allegra.

Byron's cruelty is beyond belief. Why would he enact such heartlessness? Does he wish to punish the child? Does he wish to punish Claire in some way? Does he believe her to be a bad mother; does he truly believe she is a pernicious influence on the child? He says that if the child is around Claire, Allegra will become a vegetarian and an atheist. Claire is not really like us and Byron should not make such sweeping generalizations.

I know that I find fault with Claire continually, but she does love the child and a mother's love is crucial to a child's well-being. I suffered from having no mother and although he tried, Godwin could not provide a mother's care and affection. I believe, as I've said before, that Byron himself is a wounded creature. His deformity may have turned his own mother against him and thus his heart was eternally injured and disfigured.

17 August 1818

Shelley and Claire are journeying to Venice to attempt to see Allegra and they are quite determined to plead with Byron in person. I hope to be able to join them but have felt ill of late and poor little Clara has come down with a fever. We had hoped that the mountain air and the refreshing springs would ensure continued good health, but this is not necessarily true. Clara and I have snuggled together under the eiderdown, even though it is summer. We have both had the chills and keeping Clara close to me makes me feel more secure; I know that she is warm and I hold her next to my heart.

31 August 1818

Shelley urges me to make haste to join him and Claire. Byron has relented and has agreed to allow Claire to stay for a week to visit Allegra. Of course, she is thrilled and is determined to see more of her daughter.

It appears that Shelley is having a grand time. He informs me that he and Byron have taken Byron's gondola to San Giorgio Maggiore, a nearby island, and then on to another isle, Lazzaretto Nuovo, spending two days riding through the forest and discussing their ideas for future works. Shelley feels inspired.

I am not inspired; I am tired. I do not feel that I can travel yet; our illness only recently subsided. I took Clara to a physician and he said that she was not ill but was merely teething. He reprimanded me for being a silly woman, an anxious mother, too worried about the child. I found his remarks quite belittling and patronizing and told him so. He did not apologize but merely assured me that she will be fine and that the journey will not prove too arduous for her.

10 September 1818

Byron has generously accommodated us at his villa in Este. I was quite relieved to arrive there because, despite the doctor's assurances that Clara was not ill, she had a fretful trip. She was flushed, feverish, listless, and would not eat. She occasionally shook with the ague. The carriage ride took four days and the heat was unbearable. Whenever I could, at various waystations on the journey, I applied cold compresses to her and tried to get her to take a little brandy, mostly to soothe her relentless crying. I hope that once we are settled here, she will recover from the journey and the illness.

Byron has sent for his personal physician who will likely bleed the child. I do not agree with these antiquated medical methods, straight out of Aristotle. I don't know what else to do though, if she does not recover soon.

20 September 1818

The physician, Mr. Caldona, applied leeches and took to cupping baby Clara. I hated to see him lance the hematomas that he created with the cups. The poor child cried until exhaustion and even though I held her close, her body shook as if she had palsy. I grow increasingly fretful and am angry with Shelley for insisting that we travel. He and I had a terrible row, but then we stopped our bickering when our Willmouse came in the room and told us that he was scared, could we please be quiet, he asked. I felt ashamed that we engendered fear in our sweet boy.

I haven't seen any change in my baby girl but Mr. Caldona says that we ought to see a change for the better within 24 hours. I remain by her bedside and refuse to sleep. Shelley tells me that I must but I can't. My baby remains feverish and she is difficult to arouse. I gently rub her limbs and her head and sing lullabies to her. I wish that I believed that God would intercede but I don't; I feel helpless and hopeless.

24 September 1818

The worst has happened and I fear that I will not recover. The candle has burned down and is out. Baby Clara is no more and has joined her sister Sophia in the grave. I held Clara as she took her last breaths and I wished her Godspeed. My worst fears about holding loved ones as they die have been realized. Now, I know how my mother felt when her beloved Fanny died in her arms. It is worse for me though because these babies are my own blood.

I deeply regret making this journey. Perhaps if we had stayed in Bagni di Lucca Clara could have completely recovered. I feel responsible for making a poor and selfish decision. And I blame Shelley for insisting we travel when Clara was not fully recovered. Once more, I shouted at him, calling him inhumane, cruel, and selfish. I don't know that I can ever forgive him. After our row, he stormed out and stayed away for the night. I don't know where he went and I don't care. He returned in the morning as if nothing had happened. I made the burial arrangements by myself.

At times, I feel repulsed by him and I grow increasingly angry because he does not seem to feel as despondent as I do. He carries on and continues to write. I can think of nothing but the fact that Clara's beautiful spirit has vanished.

I keep wondering what we have done to deserve such fate. Are we doomed to a relentless cycle of death? Has our passion been detrimental to us and to our offspring?

30 September 1818

After notifying Godwin about Clara's death, I received a cold letter from him, warning me not to carry on with my grief. He acknowledged that my grief is real and is the first of its kind in my adult life. (This is not true. I despaired equally when Sophia passed.) He insisted that only "persons of an ordinary sort" persist in their grief and depression and that I should apply myself to new endeavors and new thoughts if I wish to recover from this unfortunate event. His heartlessness astounds me and I grow weary of it.

I wonder about the differences between men and women in regard to coping with personal tragedy. Perhaps, since they never carried a child under their hearts, they do not feel the pain that we feel when that child is snuffed out by the gods.

I take a considerable amount of laudanum to dull the pain, but even that does not help. The emptiness inside of my chest, where my heart used to reside, is deep. I feel hollowed out from the core and have nothing to give. The reviewers of my novel labeled me mad. Like Shelley, I am mad now. But with grief.

I never was able to show my darling girl England's daffodils as I had promised. My dreams are filled with my daughters roaming through the English countryside and sitting in fields of lavender and daffodils. In the spring, I shall endeavor to locate daffodils here in Venice and place them on her grave.

15 October 1818

The beauty of Venice does not assuage my abiding grief. If anything, it exacerbates it. The canals seem fetid to me and the buildings seem ruined and crumbling. Nothing arouses hope in me.

Shelley continues his work and he encourages me to write. I cannot put pen to paper except in this journal where I can express my soul's emptiness. Every time a loved one dies, a portion of my soul dies with them.

Shelley plans for us to travel to Rome as a way to rid me of melancholy. He also wishes to study some archival materials on Cicero and for us to read Dante and Virgil together. Rome will be a new experience and, even though I suffer great emotional pain, I shall endeavor to rouse myself for the journey. I do feel distant from Shelley though and often lash out because of my anguish.

VINDICATED

8 November 1818

Claire does not realize that her ceaseless crying about her daughter only adds to my own heartache. At least her daughter lives. Mine lies in a cold, dark box. I wish Claire understood the additional grief she causes every time she weeps because of Allegra's absence.

20 November 1818

We have traveled to Rome to help lift our over-burdened hearts; as I said, mine weighs more than Shelley's, but still he grieves our loss of Clara and I know that he thinks of Ianthe and Charles continuously; he will never recover from losing them to an Anglican minister. I should be more understanding with how he copes with such tragedies. He tells me that seeing new sights will inspire us, give us hope, and add to our knowledge. It will help us with our work, which will better the world. I do agree with that sentiment and so we attempted to soothe our spirits by spending the past two days being tourists in Rome.

We explored the old city, the Roman Forum and Colosseum; we walked past the House of the Vestal Virgins, and mounted Palatine Hill. These antiquities thrilled us as we imagined what life was like during the Roman Empire. Rome certainly affected our small island and it is easy to see why with their vast roads and their splendid architecture.

The highlight for all tourists is, of course, the Trevi Fountain, which we strolled past this evening. Magnificent Neptune, Shelley's mythical father, lords over the sea as two Tritons flank him. I feel much like Mr. Wordsworth in wishing to be a pagan who believes in these anthropomorphized gods. At least they intervened in human life, for good or ill.

We learned from our guide that the fountain may have been

named after Trivia, a young girl who led thirsty Roman soldiers to the spring from which the fountain emanates. I was pleased to learn that a female guide is remembered here in relief. I tossed a coin to commemorate her leadership and to ensure a return to Rome under happier circumstances.

21 November 1818

Shelley and I went separate ways as we toured St. Peter's Basilica. He wished to spend time in the Grottoes to see the crypts of the popes, but I had no desire to dream about dead popes. Instead, I spent my time viewing the Pieta. Michelangelo's statue of the Virgin Mary cradling her dead son calms my heart. The expression of finality and acceptance on her face is admirable. However, what I admire the most is the fact that Michelangelo captured a moment in which a mother perennially holds her departed son and he is her child once again. She is like a goddess herself, maternal, matronly, with a wide lap upon which her son lays. He is hers and she will not relinquish him. This is how I interpret this masterpiece of maternal love. I imagine holding my daughters, Sophia and Clara, in this way.

Afterwards, I wandered through the basilica and gazed at the dome designed by Michelangelo. It is only the second of its kind in the world; the first is Hagia Sophia in Constantinople. Michelangelo's dome radiates like the sun itself and seems to reach to the highest heavens. I was struck by its utter splendor. The Church of England and the entire Reformation lost something when they abandoned the art and architecture of these grand basilicas and cathedrals. I know that some might think that relishing their artistry is too popish, but, to me, these extraordinary works have nothing to do with popes and their power. They are testament to the human capacity to make art, which, in my view, is what makes us human.

VINDICATED

22 November 1818

Today, we toured the Vatican art collection. I was most impressed by the Raphael Rooms, particularly the School of Athens mural, which made me wish all the more for a trip to Athens and the Agora. I now ardently wish that I could explore the Agora with my father, not with Shelley. As fellow philosophers, assuming my father thinks me one, we could walk in Plato's and Socrates's steps, but I doubt that this will ever happen. My philosophy pales in comparison to my father's.

I wandered back to our pension and stopped on the Spanish Steps and then peered down on the fountain below. Many dark-clad nuns and priests are on pilgrimage here and they were milling around the fountain, waiting for a tour. I find myself drawn to their calm demeanor, particularly when I see them praying in the cathedrals. I often wish again that I could make a confession and receive forgiveness for my transgressions and faults, particularly the injury that I caused Harriet Westbrook Shelley and the harm that I may have inadvertently caused my own daughters who could not remain in this world with me. I also seek forgiveness for the role that I played in ending my mother's life. Fortunately, my mother forgives me.

Perhaps my grief could be assuaged through a proper, heartfelt confession. Although I am not truly a Protestant, I, like Luther, make my private confession; I do not need the intercession of priestly magic to seek and receive forgiveness for my failings and indiscretions.

10 December 1818

We are in Napoli and have visited Cicero's "tomb." Together we have read Dante and Virgil again. Shelley is finally beginning what he hopes is his magnum opus, his *Prometheus Unbound*. He is certain that it will bring public scorn and hellfire on him, but, as an atheist, he cares not.

13 December 1818

This was an exceptional day because we joined a touring group that hiked up Mount Vesuvius, an active volcano, that erupted on August 24th, 79 B.C. Villas and villages were buried in ash and pumice; the eruption killed thousands of people who tried to escape their torment by racing into the sea. When I juxtapose my private grief with the sheer terror that these multitudes experienced, I realize that my grief, although profound, pales in comparison.

The trek up the volcano was about a mile long from where our cart transported us. We were able to peer into the crater but saw no lava, only steam. Nevertheless, it was a harrowing experience and Shelley kept remarking that hellfire could bubble up anytime. Peering into the abyss was like looking into hell, assuming that such a place truly exists.

A literal hell must have been realized when the volcano erupted 17 centuries ago. Of late, a new science has developed, archeology, which seeks to uncover the buried past. This site around Vesuvius is one of the major sites of exploration. The village of Pompeii is slowly being uncovered systematically and the scientists are finding cratered out areas where humans fell as the ash and pumice buried them. Children were clinging to their mothers and dogs lay beside their masters. We were told that one of the buildings that was found completely intact was a brothel, where Greek sailors found pleasure with prostitutes. Ironically, hellfire apparently had little to no effect on this pleasure palace.

28 December 1818

Our nursemaid Elise has given birth to a daughter. No one knew that she was pregnant and she claims that she didn't know but only thought that she had gained weight on the rich Italian food. We wonder who the father is. Shelley insisted that, if she is to remain in our household, she must relinquish the child to the foundling home, which she has reluctantly agreed to do.

1819

14 January 1819

Claire remains extremely unhappy and now deeply regrets surrendering Allegra to Byron. She has learned from Mrs. Hoopner, who takes Allegra to visit her father, that Byron is living his usual debauched life with his frequent sexual dalliances and his total disregard for his daughter when she does visit. If only Claire had some legal means to retrieve her child from the "good" Lord. No law protects Claire or Allegra.

Our time in Napoli remains fraught with sadness, despite all of my attempts to quash my multiple griefs. Fleeing England and its pestilence has surely not alleviated my continued pain and suffering. In fact, it may have exacerbated it.

10 February 1819

I have missed my monthly, but I dare not tell Claire who will likely be jealous and I dare not inform Shelley because he will worry about me and this pregnancy. He is busy at work on his epic drama and I continue with my plans for *Valperga*. This time in Italy may, despite my grief, be fruitful for my own work as I dream about the ruins that I visit and as I learn about the noble families who peopled the middle ages. I shall try not to fret about the outcome of this pregnancy, about which I endeavor to remain optimistic.

We will return to Rome in March and I plan to take drawing lessons, which I believe will help me visualize and write about the great cathedrals and the pre-Christian sites.

9 March 1819

Little Willmouse's Italian far exceeds his English language skills at this point. He chatters away with Elise and me. Sometimes he is mistaken for an Italian child. Italy is our adopted and spiritual home so I don't correct those who treat him as a native.

Our time is Rome has been extraordinary. In a way, I have fallen in love with it. Shelley and I visited the Pantheon at night and were profoundly moved by the moonlight as it fell through the dome. It illuminated the floor and was enhanced by the many votive candles that were lit to commemorate the dead. I lit candles for Sophia, Clara, and my mother.

Like Christopher Wren's St. Paul's, which sits on the site of a former temple dedicated to Diana, the Pantheon is an ancient Roman temple dedicated to the gods but now supplanted by the Christian god and his minions. In any case, I felt the presence of the god or gods and felt great peace within the Pantheon. Perhaps our troubles will end here and our griefs will be assuaged.

11 March 1819

Shelley wished to visit St. Peter's again and by chance we saw a rather auspicious sight. As we were perusing the basilica, the Swiss Guards walked through ordering tourists and the faithful to stand back because some dignitaries were passing through. Little did we know that we would see his Eminence, the Holy Father, the Bishop of Rome. He was only an arm's length away and he blessed the crowd as he proceeded. Again, I am not a papist but this pope, Pius VII, who was held prisoner by Napoleon, is held in high regard in Rome and throughout the Catholic world. He is considered heroic. I was glad to accept his blessing and hastily crossed myself as if I were one of his flock.

I wonder if there will ever be a female pope. I have heard of such a pope, Pope Joan, who masqueraded as a man in order to receive an education. As one would suspect, when it was discovered that she was a female and about to give birth, a mob stoned her to death. This could be an apocryphal story but it certainly seems feasible. Women cannot be popes or prime ministers or presidents, at least not in this current world.

15 March 1819

I visited the Villa Borghese and its galleries today to study Caravaggio's "Bacchus." I much prefer the "pagan" paintings to the ones that dwell on Christ's suffering. "Bacchus" seems joyous and full of life; he too, like Christ, is the god of wine and resurrection. How odd that no one acknowledges the similarities between the two gods.

8 April 1819

Shelley has introduced me to his old friend, the Irish painter Amelia Curran. Apparently, she knows my father and she and Shelley traveled together when Shelley went to Ireland to campaign for Irish Emancipation. Her sister was engaged to Robert Emmet, the Irish patriot, whom the British executed for leading what they considered a treasonous insurrection. I am quite taken with Amelia and her art and have asked her to paint our Willmouse. She has already been working on a portrait of Shelley, which is quite striking but eerily similar in its facial features to Reni's "Beatrice Cenci," Shelley's favorite painting. Beatrice is a tragic figure about whom Shelley is currently writing. I believe that he has had an effect on Amelia's work, since he has no qualms about the ways in which his face resembles Beatrice's. Perhaps Amelia sees his feminine side. Amelia has kindly agreed to give me drawing lessons.

30 April 1819

Amelia has completed Willmouse's portrait. Happily, he does not look like Beatrice Cenci! He looks very much like my own dear child. She has captured his elf-like face and demeanor and his eyes, which are truly Shelley's. She has him holding a pink rose, which droops slightly. Amelia was such a patient painter of my little man, who had a hard time sitting for his portrait, since he would rather have been chasing Alonzo the cat around the garden or kicking a ball like the other small boys in and around the pension.

5 May 1819

There is no hiding my pregnancy now, even if I wished to. I feel the child stir, like a small fish flipping its tail or a butterfly flapping its wings. I have told Shelley and he is genuinely happy. Once more, we hope for a daughter to complete our family. We are grateful for our Willmouse who delights us each day with his beautiful and loving spirit.

VINDICATED

I continue with my drawing lessons and am concentrating on still life objects, which for me are the easiest to sketch and then color; luscious grapes, black olives, and yellow roses are my objects. Amelia says after that we will work on drawing faces. I would like to be able to capture resemblances so that I can sketch a portrait of my daughter when she arrives in the late fall. I hope that by then, with sufficient practice, my skills with the drawing pencil will be much improved.

The nurse Elise has reported that Willmouse had a restless night. He woke her several times requesting water. I became cross with her because I want her to notify me if he does not feel well. She claims that he wasn't hot to the touch and this morning he appears fine, just a little tired and out of sorts, perhaps from insufficient sleep.

3 June 1819

We have sent for the physician because Will has spiked a fever and he says that his head hurts. He cries for me, "Mamma, stringimi," Mama, hold me. He wants to rest in my lap all day and he holds his stomach, telling me that his belly aches.

5 June 1819

The physician diagnosed malaria, which alarms me considerably. He told us to keep cold compresses on Willmouse and to monitor his cerebral activity. We actively try to arouse him by talking to him about Alonzo and his favorite toys, but poor Willmouse grows increasingly lethargic. The doctor has ordered quinine as the treatment and assures us that Willmouse will recover, if the drug is properly administered and if our child is faithfully monitored.

We grow increasingly worried. Despite the quinine and our constant surveillance and care, our little Willmouse has suffered several seizures from his continued high fever. He has lost consciousness several times. The quinine seems to have little to no effect. I grow distressed and do not know what to do. I begin to despair.

This evening I left the pension briefly and donned a veil to visit the Basilica di Santa Maria Maggiore. I wished to light a votive candle for my Willmouse. It briefly flickered and almost blew out, but then the flame grew strong. I dared not tell Shelley of my activity; he believes that this practice is mere superstition and magical thinking. I don't care. I would do anything to intervene on behalf of my son Will. Perhaps the pagan gods of old Roma, even Neptune, Will's mythical grandfather, will intervene.

This world seems only a quicksand. My prayers were not answered. Our Willmouse, our innocent, darling boy, is gone. This morning he suffered continuous convulsions and then did not awaken. We tried our best to rouse him, but his heart grew silent and ceased beating.

I fear that I shall indeed lose my mind and probably lose the child that I now carry, who seems doomed like all of the others. I have taken to my bed and am leaving the responsibility for the burial to Shelley and Claire. I cannot bear the thought of lowering one more child into the cold ground. My dear Amelia sits by my bedside. I have turned her portrait of Will to the wall because I cannot look at it without sobbing. I keep asking her questions she cannot answer. Why are we plagued with continuous death? What have we done to deserve this? When will it end? I know that others lose children, but we have lost three and I fear that the fourth will not remain with us. Again, I wonder if the gods are punishing us.

13 June 1819

Shelley reports that Willmouse has been interred at Cimitero Degli Ingles, the Protestant Cemetery in Rome. I now have one child buried in the watery depths of Venice, another in the cold Protestant Cemetery of Roma, and a third in merciless England. I could not leave my bed to attend the burial. The doctor has prescribed heavy doses of laudanum to control my nerves but nothing helps me sleep longer than a couple of hours. When I do sleep, I have nightmares in which Willmouse wakes in his coffin and tries to push it open. He screams from his grave and tries to claw his way out, but can't. I fear that I shall never recover from this horror. Shelley, Claire, and Amelia are patient with me. Amelia, in particular, acts like a sister to me and when I cry, she holds me close and rocks me as if I were her child.

30 June 1819

Once again we have received a severe letter from my father who advises the usual British stiff upper lip claiming that only the poor and undisciplined succumb to common melancholy. I suppose that because he never lost a child to the grave he doesn't comprehend this grief. Children should not die before their parents. That is not the natural order to things. We understand that childhood death does exist, but Willmouse had reached the age of three and was so vibrant, loving, and happy. Yet he was snuffed out so quickly and so easily. The older that he got, the more confident I felt that he would survive and grow to be a man.

I try to understand my father's callous heart. I suppose he only advises what he thinks is best, but sometimes his extreme rationality makes it seems as though he lacks a heart, even after I thought that his heart had grown. I know that he was terribly fond of my son, so he probably feels grief too, but cannot express it. I should try to be more compassionate. Even so, I suspect that he and I are not truly reconciled and that he still harbors ill feelings toward me, or he would try to console, not berate, me by calling me undisciplined.

7 July 1819

I had supposed that Shelley is not grieving as deeply as I am, but I was in error. He left a poem on my pillow. Of late, we are sleeping separately because I cannot rest at night and because my sadness is too profound. I found this poem this morning:

> (With what truth may I say –
> Roma! Roma! Roma!
> Non e più come era prima!
> It is no longer as it was before!)

> I.
> My lost William, thou in whom
> Some bright spirit lived, and did
> That decaying robe consume
> Which its lustre faintly hid, --
> Here its ashes find a tomb,
> But beneath this pyramid
> Thou art not – if a thing divine
> Like thee can die, thy funereal shrine
> Is thy mother's grief and mine.

II.
Where art thou, my gentle child?
Let me think thy spirit feeds,
With its life intense and mild,
The love of living leaves and weeds
Among these tombs and ruins wild, --
Let me think that through low seeds
Of sweet flowers and sunny grass
Into their hues and scents may pass
A portion.

I am quite moved and I must tell Shelley that I know that his grief is as profound as my own. I will rush to him and perhaps we will comfort one another.

20 July 1819

Shelley and I are reconciled; we found solace in each other's arms, but I cannot forgive my father for his hard-hearted attempt to quench my grief. My only solution is to write my way out of it. I have begun a new project, one that corresponds with Shelley's work based on the life of Beatrice Cenci, the abused Florentine girl, who murdered her father and then was executed for her crime (of course, I do not wish to murder Godwin, just chastise him).

Shelley discovered the infamous Italian story when I translated it. My story somewhat parallels Beatrice's story. In some ways, her story is my own story because it tells of a young girl, Mathilda, whose powerful and brilliant mother died when Mathilda was born and whose father was to her like a god. However, our stories diverge in that Mathilda's father, in his grief, leaves his daughter for 16 years and then returns and embraces her once again. Mathilda, like me, adores her father and wishes to spend all of her time with him, learning from him, absorbing his knowledge, conversing with him, viewing art with him, discussing Plato with him. For a brief time, he is a loving father to her but he begins to loathe a rival, a young artist named Woodville, similar to my Shelley.

When I have completed this novella, I will send it to Godwin. I wonder what his reaction will be. Of course, he will recognize us in these characters. Will this lead to a greater empathy and compassion on his part? Will he see how he found my Shelley to be his rival for my affection? Will he understand how much I loved and admired him and how I continue to mourn the loss of his love for me? Perhaps it is an exaggeration, but I feel similar to the abandoned creature whose creator loathes her.

14 August 1819

Mathilda proceeds in unexpected ways. It occurred to me that my father's love for me when I was young was at times too passionate. Is it possible that in his own grief he transferred his longing for my mother to me? Of course, there was no physical contact, but he was emotionally attached to me. He saw me as a substitute for my mother; I was her surrogate. If he couldn't have her, he would have me emotionally. Poor Mathilda's relationship with her father does cross boundaries. He, like Beatrice's father, wishes to physically connect with her in a way that is forbidden by nature. He admits his passionate love for his daughter, the love that he felt for his wife; the resemblance between Mathilda and his wife is so great that he cannot separate the two in his mind and in his emotions. Due to this forbidden, unnatural love, he decides to leave his daughter, but she follows him because she does not fully understand the nature of his desire.

I know that, like *Frankenstein*, this story touches on forbidden truths and knowledge, in this case, carnal knowledge. The story is taking on a life of its own and tells itself. I have little control over where it proceeds.

12 September 1819

Work has always been the antidote for Shelley and me, although my grief continues and my writing about father-daughter love is emotionally haunting to me. Perhaps I go too far in recognizing the most grievous of all offenses, the physical and sexual abuse of a child, but these actions do occur in families and certainly lead to the gravest consequences. My own relationship with my father was troubling at times. In so many ways, humans are wounded creatures, all of us, whether rich or poor. As a writer, I have the obligation to write the truth, in order to expose injustices, in order to begin to reform the world. I carry on my mother's work on behalf of all women. I have discussed with my mother the trajectory of this story and she endorses it. She firmly believes that truth, no matter how troubling, must be exposed, otherwise injustice will continue to prevail and a new and better world cannot be attained.

Shelley's *The Cenci*, which dwells on the same theme as *Mathilda*, is a tragic drama that he wishes to have performed at Covent Garden Theatre in London. He has written to his friend Thomas Peacock to see if he can get it staged. Peacock worries that the content is too salacious, but Shelley reminds him that Sophocles' *Oedipus Rex* confronts a similar issue and many Greek myths speak of sexual transgressions. Peacock will try again, but it may be impossible to get the drama performed. Would that our England were as fair-minded and truthful as Ancient Greece. Shelley will publish the tragedy nevertheless.

Mathilda is complete and I have sent it to Godwin for his critique.

20 September 1819

I have visited my Will's grave and I left him a pink rose. I forced myself to go and Amelia held my hand the entire way. My knees buckled as I approached and Amelia held me tight to prevent me from collapsing onto his grave. I felt relief to see a tiny etching of his dear face on his tombstone. Amelia was responsible for that. I needed to go because we are moving to Firenze soon; Shelley wishes to visit the Uffizi as do I to see the Botticelli murals, which we believe will inspire us and lend us hope. I hate to leave poor Will alone in Rome, but Amelia promises that she will visit him frequently and will act as my surrogate.

3 October 1819

On our way to Firenze, we stopped for a few days in Pisa and met, by chance, my mother's former Irish pupil, Margaret King, Lady Mont Cashell, who now goes by the name Mrs. Mason. I felt that the gods were for once looking on us favorably in perhaps arranging this happy meeting. I was thrilled to finally meet her. Godwin knows her because he has published her *Stories of Old Daniel*, a children's book, and I had heard of her for many years through my father's account of my mother's time in Ireland. What I didn't know is that Margaret participated in the Irish Rebellion when she followed Theobold Wolfe Tone and joined the Society of United Irishmen in 1798; she then fell in love with Mr. Mason and left her husband, Lord Mont Cashell. She went on to study medicine. And the only way to do that was to pretend to be a man! Like Pope Joan, she did not conform; she had to don men's clothing in order to gain knowledge and skill. She followed my mother's hope for her to be a new kind of woman.

She tells me that she only became the person that she is now because of my mother's influence. She reports, "Mary, my dear girl, your mother freed me from superstition and fear. I owe my life to her."

My heart swelled with pride to know that my mother's tutelage of Margaret, her insistence that Margaret run, jump, play, study and think, not wear whalebone stays, and dare to refuse to conform transformed Margaret's life. We never can comprehend the effects that we have on others, even if our encounters with them are brief. She has reached out to Shelley and me and promises to help us in any way that she can. She wishes to repay the loving kindness that my mother showed her. I find great solace in her presence and am grateful for the serendipity that brought us together. She has allowed me to bare my grief to her and I am exceedingly thankful for her friendship.

12 November 1819

During an excursion in the Uffizi, I felt a rush of water inside my undergarments and I told Shelley that we must make haste back to our pension. The landlady, Mrs. Bonnano, a very kind but boisterous woman, ordered her son to hurry and fetch the midwife. I think that she feared that she would have to attend the birth! However, I was in no great distress because the labor pains had not yet started, so I tried to reassure her that the birth was not imminent. When the midwife arrived, she advised that I walk around the courtyard repeatedly in order to get my womb to open and to get the child moving into the birth canal. Once the labor started in earnest, each time I felt a pain, water gushed forth onto the ground. I found this rather uncomfortable and embarrassing and I eventually returned to my confinement bed. After only a few hours, our fourth child was born. This was the easiest of the births and for once I was not wracked by fear of death. Perhaps I am now immune to the fear because death has encircled my life.

I must say that I expected and hoped for a girl, but Percy Florence was born and we are exceedingly happy and relieved. I cannot pray but I send all of my good and wholesome thoughts his way for his well-being and good health. Being born in the city of the arts is a positive omen and perhaps there is a spare "Catholic" Guardian Angel in our midst who will shield him from harm. I will not tell Shelley but I intend, when the priest is not around, to baptize Percy Florence myself in the holy fount of the Duomo di Firenze.

25 November 1819

Our Percy's looks are far different from Will's. His complexion is dark and his hair is black. He could certainly pass for an Italian bambino. He is quite easy to care for and is already sleeping for long stretches. As I did with Clara and Willmouse, I keep him close to my heart; even though Clara and Will were not unfailingly protected by my warmth, they knew that I loved them. Perhaps with the help of a Guardian Angel, I will protect him from all harm.

But just to ensure his well-being, I bundled him into a pram today and slipped into the Duomo. I have witnessed several Catholic baptisms and so knew exactly what to do. The "holy" water, it seems to me, is merely a way to acknowledge each child's sacred being. It does not work a miracle and does not cleanse away supposed original sin, a concept in which I do not believe. Instead of reciting a Christian prayer as I poured a handful of water over his head, I silently spoke a stanza from Wordsworth's "Ode to Intimations of Immortality," the stanza about "trailing clouds of glory." I believe that Percy Florence is a miracle and a gift to us. He will be my treasure and I shall safeguard him for the remainder of my life.

18 December 1819

Firenze is mad with preparations for Christmas. All of the church bells sing out at noon each day to remind the faithful to recite the Angelus. And, as usual, the bells toll the Ave Maria at sunset. There are special customs during the Christmas season though, particularly the lighting of the advent wreath, in anticipation of the birth of the Christ Child. I know that it sounds silly and superstitious but I find peace in this season. It is a way to combat the dark months and to cope, as much as possible, with the winter bleakness. Since we are pagans and not Christians, we do continue our own sort of celebration and will light the yule log as is our custom. Our Italian servants find this a bit distressing and they quickly cross themselves when we perform our pagan rituals.

1820

6 January 1820

Percy Florence grows stronger daily. He lifts his little head and has started to coo. I think that he is precocious, but Shelley reminds me that Clara and Will developed in the same way. I assert that they were also exceptional, after all they are our children and had fine intellectual pedigrees.

Percy Florence assuages my grief. Even though I miss my Sophia, Clara, and Will and shall miss them my entire life, this child is my consolation.

I have not heard a word from Godwin in regard to *Mathilda*. I shall send him another missive and ask directly for his input. Surely he has read it by now and knows whether he thinks it worthy of publication.

In the meantime, I shall devote myself to my son and when able shall return to my other Italian project, my novel *Valperga*, which has been simmering in the back of my mind for a significant amount of time.

14 February 1820

Our relationship with Mrs. Mason has grown. We write to each other frequently and she provides motherly advice to me about the care of Percy. Her medical knowledge is quite extensive and so I ask about any and all maladies that arise. She advises me in regard to what to do for the croup and how to prevent and treat mastitis. I often wish that I had met her earlier; perhaps, if I had, Sophia, Clara, and Will would still be alive. She knows the remedies for every sort of illness and she never resorts to bleeding or cupping, which she also finds barbaric. Instead, she knows all of the old ways to heal and uses herbs and tinctures that she concocts in her own apothecary. I suppose in the old days she would have been deemed a witch.

She has petitioned us to move to Pisa and I have asked Shelley about moving there to be near her. He has assured me that he will look for lodgings for us. This will also benefit his health, which has been poorly since he completed *Prometheus Unbound*. Completing his work has always taken a terrible toll on his vigor, so he is eager for a change in circumstance and the chance to be near medical help.

I am thrilled that we will be able to spend more time with Margaret who is quite content to act as a surrogate mother for Shelley and me and to be Percy's granddame. She has told me recently about how she is not able to see her own (seven) children because of her relationship with Mr. Mason and her abandonment of Lord Mont Cashell. She misses her children terribly. We can't replace them, but we can provide her with a maternal outlet.

Somehow, I believe that my own mother has sent Margaret to us, as a substitute for her physical being.

10 March 1820

We have moved to lodgings near Margaret in Pisa and are quite content. We finally feel as though we have a family again, in addition to Claire who remains with us. I still wish that her circumstances could change. Mrs. Mason is looking into finding Claire some employment, although I can't for the life of me think of anything that Claire is capable of, except perhaps giving singing lessons.

My *Valperga* continues apace. I find time to write for two hours each day. I have grown to love my heroine, Euthanasia, who believes in human rights and human liberty. She stands against her foe and former childhood friend, Castruccio. I am eager to see how she will respond to his supposed love and his amorous intent. Of course, I must abide by historical facts and I have read Machiavelli's fictionalized biography of Castracani. He epitomizes Machiavelli's belief that Might Makes Right.

It is helpful to be here in Pisa, a place that Castracani captured and where he was made imperial vicar. I speak with locals about him and the lore that remains extant about his life and his loves. The more I read and learn about him the more I see parallels between his egotism and Napoleon's; like Napoleon, he began in earnest to lead people to freedom and try to bring about peace between two opposing political parties, but then became a tyrant, even going so far as to capture and incarcerate his love.

13 April 1820

My heroine Euthanasia is at odds with what Castruccio, her love, will become. She is a loyal Florentine who defends her family and Firenze and attends both her family and her city. She cares for her blind father and learns to read Latin in order to serve him but also to ennoble her own mind. She is a form of what my mother envisioned for a woman, although a medieval version of a free and independent woman. Surely there were women in earlier eras who espoused the ability to reason and the desire for freedom for all. Although my mother was the first woman to put pen to paper about these issues, she must not have been the first to think them.

Castruccio, on the other hand, is Machiavellian in his desire to lord over regions and principalities. He does not believe in the innate goodness or intelligence of the common person and believes that he has the right and obligation to rule over them. The poor are his vassals, his inferiors. Unfortunately, he is no philosopher king, although one of his mentors, Guinigi, a former soldier turned farmer and a friend of his father's, has advised him to hold the peasant in high regard, and that, if he wishes to rule the poor, he must rule with wisdom. Castruccio listened to his advice but ignored it and decided against further education in favor of pursuing a military career. He sought fame and pugilistic power rather than wisdom. He argues with Guinigi, "Is it not fame that makes us like gods?" He will be ruled by passion rather than reason and wisdom. His passion will be detrimental to him, just as it was to my creature and to Frankenstein.

17 May 1820

Rumors fly once again in regard to our family. We have dismissed our servant Paolo who has gossiped about Claire, claiming that she gave birth to another illegitimate child and that Shelley disposed of it in a foundling home. We do not understand why Paolo would speak ill of us and spread malicious rumors. None of it is true. Claire was not even pregnant for a second time.

Shelley tells me that we must remain strong. There are always gossips that will spread all sorts of false claims and because we are writers, we will always be held in contempt, because the imagination is feared, especially in such a religious country. Nevertheless, we will travel to Livorno to consult with an attorney about these utterly false allegations. It is true that Shelley assisted an unfortunate girl who was in the "family way" and he did help her place the child in an orphanage, when her own family abandoned her.

I had greater hopes for Italian tolerance than what I see around me; England was stifling but Italy can be as well. I am aware that the townspeople of Pisa are highly superstitious. They continually worry that the devil tempts them. They believe that Lucifer walks among us. I can only say that the evil that they espouse makes devils of them.

I write about the medieval period, but some of the thinking from that era still prevails, especially in regard to hierarchical thinking and concepts of heaven and hell. However, I have found that hell can prevail right here on earth when people slander one another and when loved ones are snatched away in the blink of an eye because of our unfortunate and inherent mortality.

9 June 1820

Castruccio has achieved victory after victory and intends to vanquish the castles that remain loyal to the Guelphs, the party that opposes him and which is aligned with the papacy. My dear Euthanasia, his childhood love, will be his next victim, although he will pledge that he only desires peace for all. She, however, will assert that she will never be his slave; she will withstand his tyranny, and will never align herself with one who murders her kinsmen and friends. She desires continued independence for Firenze and Valperga.

30 June 1820

My Euthanasia appears before me daily but now a rival for Castruccio's affection, Beatrice, a beautiful prophetess and heretic, has also materialized. Sometimes I feel like a spiritualist conjuring up these figures. Although much of my novel is historical, I have completely invented these female characters, one who upholds freedom, the other who questions the Church and who will come to ponder the origin of evil.

15 July 1820

Margaret has arranged employment for Claire. She will become a governess in Firenze to a large Italian family. I can't imagine Claire as a governess. As a governess, one must be tolerant and enjoy teaching children. I have advised her to read about my mother's experience as a governess before she travels and to, at the very least, consult with Margaret in regard to the best ways to approach the occupation. I doubt that Claire will do this, but I am exceedingly grateful to Margaret, my surrogate mother, for relieving us of Claire and our responsibility for her. Perhaps Claire will become independent of us.

1 September 1820

Shelley accompanied Claire to Firenze and he left her inconsolable; he related that she couldn't stop crying and begged him to take her back home. He did not give in to her pleading. She has considerable misgivings about the venture that she has undertaken, but he assured her that all will be well and that she will find her footing.

She must win the children over, but there are five girls and three boys, a veritable brood, and she is expected to accompany them to religious services as well, which she is disinclined to do. She reminded the family that she is not Catholic, she is not even a true believer, and they say that they do not care. They just want someone to manage and discipline their children. Since Claire is much like a child herself, I expect that her employment won't last long, but I am still pleased, at long last, that she has vacated our home.

Recently, Shelley ran into an old school chum, his cousin Thomas Medwin, and has brought him to stay with us. I was hoping for quiet so that I can continue my work, but Shelley must have amusement in between his bouts of frantic writing.

On another front, our neighbors, the Gisbornes, have a son who is talking with Shelley about an entrepreneurial project that he hopes Shelley will join. His idea is to provide a steamboat service from Livorno to Marseilles. He wishes Shelley to fund it. As always, Shelley is the dreamer and he is considering it, although I caution him that our expenses are such that we can barely pay our bills and we continue to fund Godwin who has no sense at all for how to manage his finances. Shelley is just as bad as my father in his lack of fiduciary knowledge. I let Shelley dream but, if necessary, I will put a stop to any financial foolishness on his part. We do not need creditors hounding us once more!

15 October 1820

Shelley invited two more guests to our home; Professor Pacchiani from the University of Pisa who brought with him Prince

Mavrocordato of Greece, who claims to be a revolutionary. We do not care for Pacchiani; he can be very tiresome and is a bit of a charlatan, but we delight in the Prince, who is helping me with my Greek in exchange for my assistance with his English. His English is already quite splendid; he has no need of a tutor; nevertheless we have a grand time together.

13 November 1820

Our circle of friends continues to grow. Pacchiani has introduced us to a most unfortunate young girl, Emilia Viviani, whose family has sequestered her in the Convent of St. Anna. She is a member of a high-ranking Florentine family and her mother is excessively jealous of her daughter's beauty and talents and refuses to allow her to participate in society. The story itself seems almost like a fairytale. If her mother were only her stepmother, the tale would be perfect.

Shelley is enthralled with Emilia and he has every desire to free her from her captivity. Although he won't admit it, she seems another imprisoned Harriet to him, a sort of Rapunzel who must be freed from her tower. The only way that Emilia can be freed though is through a fruitful marriage, but her mother seems to wish for her to die, smothered in the convent, rather than find a suitable husband.

Emilia is confined within two small rooms and receives little physical or intellectual exercise. Shelley visits her daily to help her with her intellectual pursuits and he reads the poetry that she has written; he finds it extraordinary. I believe that he is smitten with her beauty and intellect.

I refuse to think of her as a rival. I am confident that I am Shelley's sole true love. I do not fear the game that he plays with her, but only fear that she will fall in love with him and thus may get hurt in the process.

14 December 1820

Shelley continues his daily visits to Emilia but I have refrained from visiting her. She writes to me and wonders why I have stopped calling on her, when Shelley visits. I tell her that I have my work and my Percy Florence. If I wished to visit a convent, I would seek my own vocation. I told her that in a short missive and I have heard nothing further from her.

Shelley will tire of her eventually. Besides, nothing can happen between them in the convent cell. The Mother Superior keeps a watchful eye over her charge; Emilia's mother mandates it. However, I doubt that she even knows about Shelley's daily and lengthy visits.

1821

15 January 1821

Emilia is Shelley's muse, something that I apparently have never been, even though he says that I remain his child of light. He has written "Epipsychidion" and has dedicated it to her. In some ways, Shelley views himself in the role of Dante. The longer we live in Italy the more Shelley believes he incarnates Dante.

I continue to write my novel. I also take my cues from Dante but my Beatrice is not Dante's. She's heretical but believes that she is God's handmaiden who must free women by the power of the Holy Spirit. She is able to walk through fire and people consider her a saint, but one who has renounced the papacy. She courts Castruccio whom she hopes to dissuade from war, and he is completely mesmerized by her enthralling beauty. Perhaps Shelley and Emilia resemble these characters. Beatrice is a foil for Euthanasia who, even to me, seems too good at times. I wonder what will become of these two women who have become rivals for Castruccio's love. Will they renounce him and eventually seek each other out and become companions?

16 January 1821

We have acquired new friends, Jane and Edward Williams, friends of Shelley's cousin Medwin. They have moved to Pisa to be near Medwin who supports their relationship, a relationship that is frowned upon by many, because Jane is still married to her husband John Johnson. She ran off with Edward because of Johnson's abuse of her.

Once again, we hear the same narrative of women's lives repeated again and again. This story is similar to my Aunt Eliza's story; Aunt Eliza was physically and emotionally abused by her husband and my mother saved her from being murdered by her husband.

Marriage itself often becomes, as my mother thought, a form of slavery, whereby a husband is allowed to throttle his wife without any legal repercussions. She is his property! Somehow Jane was able to flee Johnson, when he went to sea. She confided in me that at one point he tried to force her to return to him, but she had the good sense to escape his tyranny.

When will women be able to actually be free agents in their own lives and not have to worry about physical and mental abuse? When will we gain true equality? I fear that we shall never see a time when women will not fear physical violence.

VINDICATED

The Prince and I continue our lessons and I have read him portions of my novel. He is most taken with Euthanasia's philosophy and the strength of her character and will. When I remark that she seems too good, he tells me that she is an ideal woman; she may have been one of the Guardians, if she had been born in Ancient Greece. I am not sure of this. I remark, "Perhaps she is like Diotima who taught Socrates. However, Castruccio is no Socrates; he's far more of a Sophist. What do you think?" Then, the Prince laughs and we discuss the perils of sophistry.

Of late, I've noticed that Shelley keeps a watchful eye over my time with the Prince. The tables have turned, I suppose.

Shelley is more smitten with Emilia than I originally believed. I read portions of his poem and note that he calls her a "poor captive bird," his "adored Nightingale," "Seraph of Heaven! Too gentle to be human," "Thou Moon beyond the clouds!" "Thou living Form Among the Dead!" He seems a bit carried away, but it is the fifth stanza that disturbs me the most and makes my heart ache.

In it, the persona confesses, "Emily, I love thee . . . Would we two had been twins of the same mother . . . I am not thine: I am part of *thee.*"

I confess that this expression of love troubles my sensibilities and worries me. Shelley has always been passionate and his passion does prove problematic at times. I believe that I have never had a genuine rival for his affection until now. Claire tried my patience in hoping to be my rival, but she failed.

I will not make a scene though and will not even confront him. I believe that this passion will die and that he will remain mine, even if Emilia is an extraordinary beauty and a Seraph from Heaven, which I doubt.

This too shall pass and Shelley will soon return to his senses. I will never grovel for his love and affection.

Shelley has found a more suitable outlet for his expression of affection. Instead of courting Emilia himself, he plays the go-between, the Cyrano, for one of Emilia's suitors. In this way, he still confesses his love, but does so on the part of the timid young man. I am quite certain that Emilia knows that Shelley is in love with her; he told me that she read his poem. She is most likely enthralled with him too; what is not to love? All women love my Shelley.

More heartache. We have learned that our friend John Keats has died in Rome of the consumption that brought him to Rome. Poor, noble Keats. He was only 28 years old and he apparently was ill-treated by an English doctor, James Clark, who incorrectly diagnosed his disease and thought that Keats suffered, not from consumption as the doctor in London attested, but from a case of the nerves. He starved and bled Keats, much as my darling Clara was bled, but Keats ended up hemorrhaging five times on his last day of life. These cruel, barbaric practices must stop! Bleeding is not a remedy for a lung ailment or for ague or any other malady. Shelley and I are quite distraught that such a bright star in the firmament, a poet with great promise and talent, is now buried in the Protestant Cemetery in Rome where our dear Will is. If there is a God, which I sometimes doubt, he or she seems quite cruel or, at the very least, uncaring about human life. Little did I know that when I was on the Spanish Steps in Rome, Keats's deathbed was in the building directly to the right of me. He too looked down on the fountain in his last days.

We shall visit his grave when we visit our dear child's. We deeply regret the passing of our friend and had hoped that he would visit us soon. Now we shall never see him again or revel in the great promise of more poetry. Oh, that he was his immortal nightingale.

5 April 1821

I feel more confident that Shelley's amorous affections for Emilia have subsided. Keats's death may have had something to do with it, because he is mourning the loss of his friend and is beginning perhaps to understand how fleeting life can be. Also, his love for Emilia burned out quickly, when he realized that she pursued him, rather than the young swain who wishes to marry her. I learned this not from Shelley but from Claire who corresponds with Shelley. I think that she took great satisfaction in relaying to me that Shelley loved Emilia. I told her that I was well aware of his amorous affection and left it at that. Claire said nothing further, because she knows that Shelley has always preferred me to her.

I am pleased that he saw the folly of pursuing this young prisoner. Perhaps he is learning from past mistakes, although knowing him as I do, I fear that this cannot be true.

10 May 1821

Claire's drama with Byron continues. He is now living with his new mistress, the Italian Countess Guiccioli, who refuses to look after Allegra. Together they have placed Allegra in St. Anna's where Emilia resides. Byron occasionally visits the child and appears to be taken with her childish charm. He finds her quite pretty and intelligent and he tells Claire that Allegra "has a devil of a spirit" and thus finally admits that the child must be his, since she resembles him. Of course, Claire is pleased that Byron does see the child but he is severely restricting her visits with Allegra because Claire is now an avowed atheist, after everything that has happened to her. He fears that Allegra will end up like her mother and will disavow God. He wishes for Allegra to become a Catholic.

I find it most baffling that a man who is ever the libertine chooses to rely on Catholic dogma. Who would have surmised that Byron the Don Juan would align himself with Catholicism? Perhaps he has converted and sees his confessor on a weekly basis; perhaps he admits to his continual sexual license and even his perverse passion for his half-sister. I suppose that he receives absolution and then feels free to sin again.

Shelley and I do our best to assure Claire that Allegra is being well cared for and is beginning to receive an education, although we have not witnessed or seen the way that girls are educated in this convent.

20 May 1821

The Prince reports tremendous news from Greece. A Greek general, Ipselanti, has led 10,000 Greeks into battle against the Ottoman Empire and they have apparently won the battle. Prince Mavrocordato is ecstatic! We celebrated the victory by drinking Greek Ouzo. As I said, I am not an imbiber, but I was happy to drink one round with my friend to celebrate. It gave me great hope that all empires will eventually fall, as Shelley and I have long hoped. His "Ozymandias" is based on this supposition. We continue to believe in ultimate human freedom from all tyranny whether national, religious, or ideological.

VINDICATED

13 June 1821

Valperga continues and is inspired by the news from Greece. Euthanasia stood up to Castruccio, the prince, and imperial vicar, but he destroyed her castle and then imprisoned her because she plotted against him. Beatrice, the supposed saint, has died, after succumbing to madness. She continued to love Castruccio, despite his malignant acts. Now, Euthanasia is imprisoned in Lucca and Castruccio repents of his treatment of her and offers to free her. She wishes her co-conspirators to be freed also, but he refuses. Although she does feel profound love for the man that Castruccio formerly was, she tells him that she does not recognize the man that he has become. He is alien to her. He has become a tyrant and even if he professes love of her, how can he treat her countrymen as he does? After all, he has slaughtered them. She says that she would rather live in a convent than become his wife; she would rather retreat to a far-flung island than to share his bed. She is a bold woman who desires liberty and justice.

10 September 1821

The Williamses have become close friends with Shelley. Edward and Shelley spend vast amounts of time together. They have designed a sail boat that they plan to have built. Shelley will be back in his element; he will be a merman once again.

Jane Williams delights Shelley with her sparkling and lilting singing voice. Her singing rivals Claire's. She could be an opera star, but she learns many Italian folk songs and sings them to Percy Florence.

We feel profoundly content at this moment. Nothing seems awry; trouble seems distant. Perhaps it will stay away and leave us alone for once.

5 October 1821

Claire continues to work as a governess, although she has become increasingly nervous about Allegra's physical condition and her confinement in St. Anna's. She thinks that Allegra's health is fragile and has even confided to me her plans to kidnap the child and run away with her this spring! I am reminded of the time that Claire told her mother that she would break out of a convent if confined. Now, she falsely believes that she can penetrate a convent's walls.

I have written to Claire that this plan of hers is sheer madness, an utter absurdity. First of all, how would she gain access to the convent? Its walls are ten feet high and its entrances are locked at all times. One must seek permission to enter. Second, if she did penetrate the walls and seize the child, what would she do with her? How would she support her? As always, Claire has no legal advantage and cannot feasibly support the child on her governess salary. Plus, the family that she works for would not allow her to keep the child in their home. Third, Byron would certainly find Claire no matter where she went with Allegra. He has ready silver at his disposal; he could hire a detective and has already relayed that if Claire annoys him further, he will take Allegra and hide her; Claire will never see her again.

I await Claire's reply. Surely, she must see reason.

15 November 1821

Claire holds out hope that she can retrieve Allegra from the convent. This time I have been very direct with her and told her to please desist in her plan. Spring is always our unlucky time of the year. She knows that many troubles have befallen us when the season changes. I can't explain why the black cloud that overhangs us always rains down on us in the spring. The Chancery suit, the slander from Paolo, her acquaintance with Byron, our misery in Rome with poor Will's illness and death . . . I could go on, but don't care to relive every misery that has befallen us in the spring.

20 December 1821

I hear no more from Claire about her ill-fated plan. If she brings it up again, I intend to warn her that her plan may compel Shelley to confront Byron in a physical manner. Perhaps he would even be forced to fight a duel with him. Shelley has a vehement temper but Byron is a practiced military man who has often fought duels. He has not missed his mark. Would she want to endanger Shelley whom she has long loved? Surely, she would not want to pose this threat.

Of course, I know for a fact that Shelley would never fight Byron in a duel. He knows, as Caroline Lamb attests, that Byron is "mad, bad, and dangerous to know." We are all a little frightened of the lord. And, although he dislikes Byron's morals and finds Byron appalling at times, Shelley greatly admires his poetry and intellect. He enjoys conversing with him and even arguing with him about our tangled lives. He does verbally defend Claire to Byron but it is doubtful that he would physically defend her, if he were called upon to defend her honor. Despite his occasional madness, he has better sense than that.

1822

19 January 1822

I am about to complete *Valperga*, which has been quite gratifying to me as I see the connections between our tumultuous time and struggle for independence and a similar medieval scenario. Euthanasia's heart has nearly overridden her reason in her desire to love Castruccio as she once did. As she works out her destiny, she has decided that she can never love him again or let him lord over her. She will sail away on her "Ariel" and hence will flee her tyrant who claims to love her. Like my poor, friendless creature in *Frankenstein*, I see an unfortunate end in sight for her. She may wish to escape patriarchy but cannot, unless she were to set up her own utopian space where no men can reside. She may long for that and had believed that her fortress was impenetrable from harm and yet it was not so. I see her seeking a remote island but I feel certain that she shall not arrive safely. She does not possess Shelley's superior marine skills and I see a tempest on the horizon.

13 February 1822

Valperga is finished. Much to my dismay, once it is published, I will give the proceeds to Godwin who continues to suffer financial crisis. I wish that Godwin showed more gratitude. He never responded to my query about *Mathilda* and will probably neglect this novel also. I, on the other hand, have read every word that he has ever written.

8 March 1822

Shelley and Edward Williams have plans to create a writers colony. They intend to invite the Hunts to join us and we already have Margaret King Mason nearby. She is quite interested in perhaps becoming a member, since she is a celebrated author of several children's books.

Shelley says that he grows sick of Byron; if that is the case, I asked him why he and Edward plan to name the new boat that they have ordered "Don Juan." Shelley says that it is not in homage to Byron but is merely a lark. I don't find it amusing.

Of late, I have felt somewhat estranged from Shelley who is once again in a flirtatious mood, but this time with Jane Williams. He becomes quite captivated with singers and cannot control his lust. I often wonder if it is like that Italian folktale about the opera singer, Farinelli, who enchants his listeners, but whose voice is wicked and emanates from evil; ultimately, if you hear his song for the third time, you will die. I doubt that this will happen to Shelley but he spends much time listening to Jane's voice, which is clear, high, and beautifully wicked. I warn him to refrain from listening to a song thrice, but he ignores my advice.

25 March 1822

It is highly ironic that I now find myself with child once again; Shelley and I have grown apart and we are often at odds with one another. I try my best to refrain from jealousy but I do not care for his attention to Jane who enjoys his flirtations and whose husband seems oblivious of the emotional connection between Shelley and Jane.

I must always remind myself that Shelley chose me and, to my knowledge, has never engaged in any sexual intimacy with any one of his numerous "loves." He tells me that each of these women have served as muses. Why is it that I have not?

26 April 1822

As I predicted, spring is once more unlucky for us. Claire has received devastating news about Allegra. Shelley had to inform her that Allegra died of typhus. Claire is now accusing Byron of murdering her child through neglect and through confining her in that pestilence-ridden convent. Byron has told Shelley that he will bury the child in England on his estate and he now regrets that he had not visited her in many months.

I fear that Claire will go mad. I do know and understand her grief, since I have been the victim of it numerous times, first Sophia, then Clara, then my Willmouse. I cling to my dear Percy Florence who, thank God, remains healthy.

7 May 1822

I have visited Claire who is quite despondent. Nothing has turned out as she had hoped. Byron never loved her or their child. Ironically, her relationship with Bryon is somewhat similar to my mother's and Imlay's, although Byron never suggested a ménage a trois. If he had, I am certain that Claire would have embraced the notion, even though towards the end of their acquaintance, she often said that she completely loathed him and realized that he is the devil incarnate.

Byron insisted that Allegra be educated as an Italian Catholic, believing that with this education she would one day be able to marry into Italian nobility. Claire was completely opposed to this and had told Byron many times that such an education would make Allegra subservient. Now, the child is dead and Claire is certain that the child had completely forgotten about her. Like me, she has nightmares about her child calling for her from her grave.

Claire has been quite an actress but this time her theatrics have some substance. I do feel for my stepsister and wish that I could calm her but I fear that she shall never recover from this unnatural event.

VINDICATED

10 May 1822

Claire has returned to us and we have moved to Casa Magni in San Terenzo. Shelley is thrilled that the sailboat that he has designed has arrived; he *has* named it Don Juan. He plans to sail alone beyond Livorno and out into the sea. He, of course, is Neptune's son and is an able sailor. I have no worries about his solitary sailing.

1 June 1822

Shelley has renamed his vessel Ariel; I believe that he finally decided after Allegra's death that he wishes to part with Byron. I do not oppose this renaming nor do I oppose separating ourselves from Byron who has been heartless throughout this entire ordeal.

Perhaps in naming the bark Ariel, Shelley will throw a girdle around the world and will work sufficient magic to preclude us from more harm. Clearly, Shakespeare's Ariel quelled tempests and brought about a good end for all, including himself who was finally freed from Prospero's tyranny.

16 June 1822

I awoke last evening to cramping and the bed sheets were saturated with blood. I cried out and Shelley called for Elise to help me. She lifted my legs but the bleeding would not stop. Finally, Shelley retrieved a large bucket of ice and advised me to sit in it. I cried the entire time and felt certain that I, like my mother, would join Fanny Blood. Shelley held me as I sat in my own blood and once the bleeding stopped we found a tiny creature in among the liquid. Whether female or male we could not tell. We both cried when we saw the creature who was not destined to live in this world.

Shelley held me all night and I found comfort in knowing that his love for me is intact.

22 June 1822

I provided comfort for my Shelley tonight. I have just now calmed him after he woke me with his screams. "Mary, my darling," he cried. "I just had the most wretched vision. I saw Edward walk naked into our room, his skin was bloodied and torn. Edward told me to get up quickly because the sea is flooding the house." It took all of my effort to assure him that Edward was safe in his villa and that the sea had not swamped ours. I believe that as I spoke with him he was still dreaming his nightmarish vision.

After I managed to get Shelley subdued, I went out on the balcony and looked at the sea, which was quite serene. I felt comforted that Shelley's vision was merely a bad dream, probably related to our most recent tragedies.

24 June 1822

Jane Williams came to me today and told me about another disquieting event. She claims that she saw Shelley walking on her terrace two evenings ago, but he was not in their house. He was at home with me.

All of us seem on edge and I cannot understand why, other than because of the loss of our child. Even so, Shelley has returned to work and continues to pursue his vision to create a writers colony. The Hunts have safely arrived in Livorno and he and Edward plan to sail to meet them on 1 July.

Of late, my sleep is dreamless, just like my creature's. I miss my mother's counsel. But I am thankful that I am not plagued by waking nightmares, as Shelley and Jane seemingly are. If I were, I fear that we would all go mad.

VINDICATED

I wished Shelley Godspeed as he and Edward set off for Livorno. The sky is robin-egg blue and winds are fair; no doubt, they shall have a good sail. Before they left, Shelley ironically spoke lines from his "Ode to the West Wind." I told him that such words were not entirely appropriate but he just laughed and kissed me on the forehead, telling me that the winds favor them, as do the gods. Of course, he does not believe in the gods so their favor means nothing.

Shelley and Edward say that they will return on 8 July and after that we shall have our writers colony; we will create our own world, our own garden á la Voltaire. I have no need of a writers colony. I work alone generally, but I do understand the need for solidarity and the re-creation of community and society based on freedom and imagination.

6 July 1822

I received a tender letter from my Shelley who inquired about my health and Percy's health. He asked me not to grieve too much for the child that I lost. It was not meant to be. He tells me that he has located the translation of the *Symposium* for which he was searching and that he will be home soon.

8 July 1822

Like Penelope, Jane and I eagerly await the return of our two seafarers to Casa Magni. But we sense that they have not set sail because a gale has arisen; the tempest continues all day and we must remain indoors.

To pass the time, Percy Florence and I wrote a short story based on one of his favorite inventions, Timothy the Mouse, which reminds me of our lost Willmouse. I write the story that he dictates and he likes for me to draw the figure that he has in his mind's eye. My drawing lessons from Amelia have paid off and my mouse is a fair rodent.

10 July 1822

Still no word about Shelley and Edward. We feel assured that they holed up because of the storm and that now that the weather is calm and the sky is blue once more, the billowing sails on Ariel will appear and deliver our "good spirits" to their home, leaving the harpies behind.

13 July 1822

No Shelley yet. We did receive an alarming post from Hunt today though, asking Shelley if he arrived home safely. We now know that Shelley and Edward sailed into fair weather, but then a storm arose on Monday.

I will not succumb to despair. Our friend Edward Trelawny will travel the route to Livorno and will try to find Edward and Shelley. He assures me that they are probably sitting drenched in a pub drinking spirits by the fireside and have not had a chance to send us news that they are safe and will be home soon.

EPILOGUE

1835

It had been years since I had seen it. As I was packing Percy Florence's trunk to prepare to return him for the schoolyear to Harrow, I was sorting through clothes in his armoire and found my journal buried beneath one of his frock coats. I recall hiding the journal in an old chest so that I wouldn't be tempted to look at it and be reminded, but now, somehow, Percy had purloined it and presumably read it. I always intended to keep my thoughts private, except for that which I deliberately published. At first, knowing that he read it without my permission, I grew angry, but then remembered how Godwin had forbidden me from reading my mother's memoir and then I recalled how I read *everything* that I could about my own mother, in order to know her. At least, in this case, he had my own words, not someone else's narrative and partial truth. Percy deserved to know the entire truth about Shelley and me and now he does. I should not berate him for wanting to know more, for after all, he's not a child; he is sixteen, the same age I was when I ran off with Shelley.

I opened the journal with great apprehension, because I feared meeting my young self on the page, Mary Wollstonecraft's and William Godwin's only child, Shelley's idealistic "child of light." I discovered the journal late in the evening and I retreated to my room to read it. I let the candle burn all of the way down before I completed my reading. I sobbed as I read my reactions to Sophia's, Clara's, and Will's deaths. Sophia would have been 19 this year, Will 18, Clara 17. I closed the book as I read Trelawny's assurance that my Shelley and Edward were ensconced in a pub as they prepared to write to us to tell us that they had survived a tempest. They had not. My Beloved Shelley, despite his brilliance, was ever the mad fool. He believed that he could, like Prospero, withstand a tempest but alas he could not work magic, as Ariel had, and throw a girdle around the world.

I did not speak to Percy about his piracy and how he intruded on my privacy but instead decided to ask if he would like to travel with me to Italy. We would delay sending him back to school. He had never been back to his birthplace and I finally felt able to return to that land that stole Shelley from me. I was ready to confront the pain by visiting the site of Shelley's drowning. Then we would travel to Rome to the Protestant Cemetery, then to Lake Geneva and Villa Diodati to see where his father and I spent our happiest and most productive times. "Indeed, Mother," he said cheerfully. "I wish to know all I can about you and Father." He didn't bother to confess that he knew about our elopement, Shelley's occasional madness, the death of his siblings, or the way that Claire lusted after my husband, or even the fact that some believed that I had killed my mother.

VINDICATED

I hoped that a return to Italy would quell my pain for good and bestow a sense of peace. And it was time for Percy to learn what happened on the Ligurian Sea.

We traveled to Viareggio and I directed the driver to the beach north of the village. I dismissed him and then took Percy's arm and we strolled on the beach. As we walked along the shoreline, we watched as terns and sandpipers raced the tide back and forth as it ebbed and flowed. Grey clouds dotted the sky. In the distance, we could see the Apuan Alps. A child was building a sandcastle too near the water; it was constantly getting washed away, other children and their parents were digging for shells. We saw couples amble by with parasols unfurled. Gentlemen tipped their hats to us as their ladies greeted us. "Ciao," they said, as they nodded their heads.

I had never been to this beach. When Shelley's body washed ashore here, I relied on Trelawny and Byron to arrange his internment. At the time, I was so distraught that I kept to my bed for weeks; I couldn't eat; I felt physically ill; I couldn't sleep without heavy doses of laudanum. I couldn't grasp what had happened. My Shelley, my merman, was drowned. I would never see or speak to him again. I would never feel his arms surround and comfort me. And, unlike my mother, he never visited me in my dreams. I missed him and wept until I could no longer produce tears.

Weeks later, I read the dreadful notice in *The Courier*, which Mrs. Clairmont had sent me. "Shelley, the writer of some infidel poetry, has been drowned; now he knows whether there is God or no." When I read that hateful, misguided remark, I threw the newspaper in the fire and vowed to redeem his image. The world would know Shelley as I knew him; as a great poet, a seeker and explorer of infinite worlds. God and Mrs. Clairmont be damned.

I was lost in my reverie when Percy asked, "Why are we here, Mother? Did you and Father visit this beach when we lived in Italy?"

"No, Percy, I've never been here." I paused and turned toward him. "This is where your father's body washed ashore." Percy looked shaken and surprised. I pulled him closer to me and pointed toward the sea. "Out there, a few miles out, is where the Ariel, their sailboat, capsized. It's hard to imagine, isn't it, that this is the same sea that took your father's life?" Percy and I looked out at the placid water that was Shelley's graveyard. "I needed to come here to see where it all occurred. I hope that this doesn't trouble you too much, my darling."

"I am fine, Mother. I was just a child and have no memory of his death. I only recall that my nurse, Elise, spent a lot of time with me, because you were so sad. I tried to cheer you up sometimes by singing you silly songs."

"I remember, Percy. That was inordinately sweet. You've always been a great comfort to me." I held his arm tighter and interlaced my fingers with his.

We were quiet for a long while and then Percy continued, "Mother, is it true, as I've heard whispered at school—that Father deliberately set out to die?"

"What? That's absurd. Who said that?" I thought of all the rumors that had swirled around Shelley and me and now, even in death, the gossipers could not resist maligning us. I also remembered that Percy read in my journal that Shelley *had* threatened to kill himself if I did not elope with him.

"Some boys who wish to taunt me," he replied.

"You must ignore those heartless boys. Your father loved us. He loved life, even if our lives were sometimes troubled. He would never have purposefully set out to die. He was just foolish and believed that he could sail through a frightful storm. He wanted to come home. He missed us." My heart ached with the thought that anyone would believe that Shelley was depressed and suicidal, least of all Percy Florence.

"But, what shall I tell those boys, if they belittle our family by calling Father a suicide?" He dared not look me in the face. He picked up a stick from the beach and started to dig in the sand as if he were hunting for buried treasure; perhaps he thought that after all these years, on this beach, he'd find a remnant of his father: a ring, a watch, a lock of hair.

"You should tell them that your father was a great poet who wished to transform the world. He was an old soul who could not abide tyranny. You understand that, yes?"

"Of course, Mother. I've read all of Father's work and I've learned some of it by heart."

"Oh, I didn't know that. I am so pleased." I gave his hand a squeeze.

We sat on the seawall and then I said, "I've brought you here so that we could remember Shelley and memorialize him. Let's not discuss the gossipers and those who were jealous of Shelley's gifts. Let's think about your father. We will go to Rome to see where his ashes rest but before we travel there, I want you to know what I had engraved on his tomb. It says 'Cor Cordium' and below 'Ariel's Song' is inscribed. They were his favorite verses in Shakespeare." I began,

> Full fathom five thy father lies;
> Of his bones are coral made;
> Those are pearls that were his eyes:
> Nothing of him that doth fade,
> But doth suffer a sea-change
> Into something rich and strange.

"Those are my favorite lines too," Percy said and then he asked, "May *I* read something, Mother?"

"Oh, you've written something?"

"No, of course not," he said. His cheeks flushed. "You know I am not a poet. But I admire Father's work and I know that Father wrote this for Keats, but it seems fitting to read it here and now. I always carry this poem with me. He pulled out a sheet of paper from his waistcoat breast pocket and began to read,

> I weep for Adonais—he is dead!
> Oh, weep for Adonais! Though our tears

but then he placed the paper on the sand. He continued from his heart,

> Thaw not the frost which binds so dear a
> Head!
> With me
> Died Adonais; till the Future dares
> Forget the Past, his fate and fame shall be
> An echo and a light unto eternity!

I was so moved that my son knew by heart his father's poem, a perfect commemoration of him. "Thank you, my darling," I replied, as tears swelled and then gushed from my eyes. Percy quickly pulled his handkerchief from his label pocket and wiped my tears. Suddenly, a gust of wind blew the poem into the sea and I grabbed Percy's arm as he lurched to retrieve it. "Let it go, love," I advised.

Percy wiped his own tears with the back of his hand and then I said, "I think that you're ready to hear what happened here. Are you ready to learn what happened to your father?" He nodded and then my voice shook as I began to tell the tale.

"On July 8th your father and Edward Williams set sail to return to us in San Terenzo. The day was fair; the winds were calm, just like today. They had hired a young swain to help with the large masts. They were eager to get home to start their writers colony here in this paradise and they no doubt discussed their plans as they sailed. Suddenly, though, a squall came up. According to Trelawny, a fisherman saw the masts lilt and then topple. The boy, who was up on the largest mast, was thrown into the sea. The fisherman raced toward them but could not reach the Ariel before it capsized. It must have quickly sank, because when Trelawny found Shelley's and Edward's bodies, they were still wearing their boots."

I saw Percy flinch but I needed to continue before I lost my nerve. "They had little to no time to save themselves. Trelawny was horrified when he saw them. The only way that he could initially identify them was through their clothing. Your father was so disfigured by the sea and the sea creatures who fed on his body that he was mostly unrecognizable. Percy, Trelawny said that your father's comely face was eaten away," I cried. "The only way he was assured that this corpse was Shelley is that Trelawny found a copy of Keats's poems, 'Lamia, Isabella,' in the pocket of Shelley's coat. He always carried those poems near his heart."

I looked at my son. He said nothing but stared at the horizon. The wind had suddenly picked up and storm clouds gathered above us. In the distance, we heard heat lightning.

"Trelawny wished to take Shelley's and Edward's bodies back to our village for a proper burial but local authorities insisted that they be interred here. But then someone decided that their bodies contained contagion because they had been in the sea for days. Percy, my darling, the Italian authorities insisted that they be dug up and then burned on the beach. Your father, like my creature, was the victim of an unholy conflagration!"

"Oh, Mother, I didn't know. I am so sorry. That must have been dreadful for you. Did you witness it?"

"No, I couldn't leave my bed and I couldn't bear to watch your father be burnt. Trelawny and Byron witnessed it, but Byron was so overcome with his own grief, that he disrobed and then he swam out to sea before they placed your father on the flames. Are you certain that you want me to proceed? There's more to tell that may disturb you."

"No, tell all. I need to know. I am not a child." He sat up straighter and threw back his shoulders. "Please do go on."

I took a breath and tried to steady myself, "The authorities built a funeral pyre and before your father's and Edward's bodies were placed on it, Trelawny performed a ceremony of sorts. Like a pagan priest, he poured frankincense, salt, and wine on their bodies and then read some of Shelley's poems. Crowds gathered to watch the cremation as if it were a spectacle, a carnival. People seemed to think that this ceremony was some sort of entertainment. Then as Trelawny watched the guards place your father on the funeral pyre, he raced toward them and snatched Shelley's heart from the flames. He burned his hands retrieving your father's heart. Then he watched as your father's body was consumed in flames. He waited until the flames went out and the embers died down and then he gathered his ashes.

Afterwards, he came to me and handed me a bag that contained Shelley's ashes and then he said, 'I have something else for you.'

'What is it? What have you brought me?' I asked. I thought of Keats's poems or perhaps a lock of Shelley's dark hair.

'I saved his heart for you;' he thrust a second, smaller bag toward me.

I pushed his hand away and recoiled. 'What? No, please, I cannot. I don't want it. I don't need it,' I cried. 'I know that you mean well, Edward, but what good will his drowned heart do me?'

'I thought that it would bring you comfort,' he said.

'No, it will bring me great suffering. I cannot look at it. Please, Edward, take it away,' I replied.

Percy didn't respond, but after a short while, he asked, "What happened to his heart?"

"At a later time, Trelawny, under my instruction, buried it at the family's estate that you will one day inherit."

"Well, at least his heart remains in England," Percy said.

I didn't tell Percy Florence the entire truth about Shelley's heart, for I asked Trelawny to please burn Shelley's heart quickly and dispose of it. What good would it do for me to possess his material heart? I knew that I possessed it when he was alive, ever since I was 16 years old. His drowned heart would not serve me in any fashion. Trelawny did as I requested and then spread the ashes here in this sea that killed him.

I then told Percy Florence about his father's premonitions and how they came true and then how later the night that he was found, I dreamt about another storm in which he nearly drowned in 1816, when his boatman held the sail too long and then finally let go. "Shelley was terrified as the waves swamped the boat but he tried and succeeding in saving his companion from being tossed overboard. In my dream, I saw him save his friend. I feel assured that he did his best to try and save Edward when the Ariel sank because, even though impetuous, he was always a brave man who never allowed others to suffer."

Percy gathered me in his arms and said, "Mother, I am grateful that you shared this story with me. But I know that you suffered as you told it."

"In truth, darling, I suffered more by keeping the story buried for nearly two decades in my own heart," I replied. In telling the story, I had released it.

Just then the storm clouds began to dissipate and the sun peaked from behind a cloud. A nightingale sang and then flew over our heads. I looked at Percy and he seemed bathed in light, as if he were *my* child of light. I hugged him tightly to me and we sat for a long while watching the waves baptize the shore.

After Shelley's ashes were interred in the Protestant Cemetery in Rome next to our darling boy, our Willmouse, and near our friend Keats, Claire arrived to console me, but she wept bitterly and she mostly kept to her room. She wore black as I did. One evening when she came down to dinner, she was wearing a widow's cap. I told her that I was his widow, not her. "Take it off," I ordered. She did as I said, but then raced to her room. In the morning, she left and I didn't see her again. She remained on the continent and worked as a ladies' companion. She never married.

Afterwards Percy Florence and I returned to England, which, although fraught with a history of troubles for us, made the most sense, because I could not bear to spend more time in Italy, the scene of Shelley's, Will's, and Clara's deaths, even though it was our spiritual home. Regretfully, I left behind my dear surrogate mother, Margaret King, but knew that it was necessary to return to my birthplace and to my father.

Because of Shelley's death, my father and I reconciled. While I was still in Italy, he encouraged me to come home, "I suppose [now] you can hardly stay in Italy. In that case, we will be near to, and support each other." Once I returned to England, we spent much time in each other's company and recently, we traveled to

VINDICATED

Athens, as I had always hoped, and walked in the Agora to trace Plato's and Socrates's steps.

I recall my conversation with my father when we were outside the Temple of Hephaestus at night in the Agora. The sky was cloudless and Ursa Major and Orion were profoundly bright.

"Mary, do you recollect the story that Socrates told of Thales, the first philosopher? How he gazed at the stars so intently and for so long as he walked that he fell down a well?"

I laughed and turned my attention from the stars to my father, "Yes, of course, I've read that story countless times. Why do you mention it?"

"Thales was perhaps foolish but Socrates failed to understand that sometimes falling into a well from gazing at the stars, contemplating the difficult and paradoxical questions, can transport you to a different world. A better world where truth prevails. Your mother and I understood that, but you're the star-gazer who realized that."

My heart skipped a little beat and I hesitated and then asked, "What are you implying, Father? What have I realized?"

"Dear child, I need you to know that from the beginning of your writing career, I've approved of all that you've written. You achieved what other philosophers could not. Your mother and I were your guides, but you found a new world for all of us, one based on ethical and moral principles about the potentials of the new science and one based on just and righteous principles between humans. You wrote about the need not just for reason to prevail over passion, but for humans to have compassion and love for their fellow creatures. I am indeed proud that you are my daughter. You're the philosopher that I hoped you would be. I may be an old Prospero buried in my books but you are certainly the new Miranda who truly imagines the beginning of a new world. You, not I, have worked magic."

My vision clouded over and I wiped moisture from my eyes. I tried to speak but couldn't. Then, Godwin reached for my hand and we walked arm in arm out of the Agora into that new world.

With my father's blessing, I remained a widow. I wore widow's weeds for years, even though I received numerous marriage proposals, including an expression of love from the popular American author Washington Irving. Father knew that no one could replace my Shelley, who had owned my heart since I was 16 years old.

Since Shelley's death, I have survived and lived because of my pen. I published three more philosophical novels and wrote biographies of literary and scientific men. I worked as a translator, remembering Keats's implication that translation is an art, not a transcription. I gathered Shelley's poems, edited, and published them so that the world would know him, not as a heretic, but as a believer in human perfectibility.

Despite my creature's hideousness, *Frankenstein* has enjoyed considerable success; it has even been transformed into a play, H.M. Milner's *Frankenstein, or The Demon of Switzerland* and has been performed frequently. I've been delighted to witness performances, although Milner has taken great license and has morphed my neglected creature into an inarticulate monster who lacks a conscience or a soul. This displeases me but I understand that I have no control of my own creation, which now has taken on a life of its own.

Although women have not yet attained full and equal rights, I believe that over the course of my life I have fostered my mother's goals. Although educated and raised by my father, I have always been my mother's disciple, ever since I read her work at her grave. Like my mother, I pursued intellectual and artistic endeavors to prove women's humanity and equality. Like my mother, I dreamt of a new world for women. Like my mother, I held on to my highest ideals despite endless hardship and heartache. I did this despite the universe's attempt to kill my very soul each time each beloved child died and left me to grieve. I withstood the universe's last attempt to annihilate me, when it stole my beloved Shelley from me.

I feel vindicated as I sit on the veranda here at Villa Diodati. The ghosts of Shelley and Byron haunt this place. Byron passed two years after my Shelley, playing the hero that he always envisioned himself as. I sit and watch the sailboats glide past. I see my Shelley, my Merman, manning one of them as he converses with Lord Byron. I see my children, Sophia, Clara, and Willmouse, in the bark with Shelley as they listen eagerly to Shelley's stories and dreams of a perfect heaven right here on this blessed earth. Percy Florence sits by my side in this garden and is my sole earthly consolation. Unfortunately, my daughters did not live to help create this new world for all of us. Yet, even so, my ghostly mother sits next to me, as she always has, and she places her warm hand in mine. Her hand continues to guide mine, as I pick up my pen once more.

About the Author

Kathleen Williams Renk taught British and Women's literature for nearly three decades in the United States and abroad. Her scholarly books include *Magic, Science, and Empire in Postcolonial Literature: The Alchemical Literary Imagination* (2012), and *Women Writing the Neo-Victorian Novel: Erotic "Victorians"* (2020). Renk studied fiction writing at the University of Iowa with Pulitzer Prize-winning author James Alan MacPherson. Her short fiction and creative nonfiction have appeared in *Iowa City Magazine, Literary Yard, Page and Spine*, and *CC & D Magazine*. *Vindicated* is her first novel.